SWINDLER & SON

A HEIST MISADVENTURE

by

Ted Krever

Little David Publications

www.tedkrever.com

~~~~

ISBN: 978-1-7327865-4-7

~~~~

Cover painting by Da Vinci, public domain

Graffiti by author

~~~~

Author Photo by CO Moed,

used with permission

ADVANCE PRAISE

FOR

'SWINDLER & SON'

"Ted Krever is an amazing storyteller and brilliantly weaves a tale of intrigue that, like our insane world, is all too real." - David Leaf, Producer of 'The US vs. John Lennon' and author of 'The Beach Boys and the California Myth.'

"I rate this book 5 stars with a strong recommendation to begin reading in the morning because you won't put it down until you reach the end...hits the ground running and doesn't let the reader catch a breath until the very end.

...a phenomenal plot with a horrific idea thrown in for good measure. However, the heart of the book is about love, don't let the amount of guns and ammunition certain soldiers are carrying fool you. This is about a son's love for his not-father and a couple who ricochet (bad, really bad choice of words) off each other better than they would off a wall.

Krever's characters...are all created with heart and jolly good humour...Like all good authors, I didn't have to try to read a character, the character was shown to me.

'"Great fun read...everyone likes a happy ending. Super holiday reading. Thoroughly recommended." - 5 Stars!

"I grew to love Nick as a person...he resonated, as did Harry and Sara and a host of others." - 4 Stars!

"...international adventure, political intrigue and some creative interpretation of the facts. All in the name of the game, love and friendship...although no one says no to money either." - 4 Stars!

"...a page-turning romp through the seamier side of life...."

"...funny, delicious and gripping..."

OTHER BOOKS BY TED KREVER:

Mindbenders

Mindbenders 2: The Fiery Sky

Green

A Crafty and Devious God

Howling at Wolves

After

'Did you torture him?'
Captain Segura laughed. 'No. He doesn't belong to the torturable class.'

- *Our Man In Havana*, Graham Greene

THE START

-So how does it start?

It starts with the sound of my own name spoken aloud.

Call me Nicholas, I'm fine. Nick or Nicky, even better.

But 'Nicholas Marsh' enunciated, first and last, all the way through—when I hear it *that* way, I know I've done something I'm about to pay for.

Hearing it in French, every syllable twisted and slurred and leaking from the earpiece of a Parisian counterterrorism officer in a Kevlar vest, his back to me and his binoculars trained on my kitchen window—*that's* rock-bottom.

That's how it starts, in the snowy garden of the *Hopital Saint-Louis* in the Tenth Arrondissement, just past sundown on Christmas day, at what I fervently hoped was the end of one of the worst days of my life.

Well, actually, no...

Actually, it started about fifteen minutes earlier, on the other side of the canal, where I was mugged by some twenty-five-year-old junkie in a purple-tinted mohawk and a leather jacket. And several nice tats on his neck that distracted my attention when I should have been focusing on his oncoming fist. He took my wallet and phone and left me aching and dizzy, which is why I wandered groggy several blocks out of my way and approached home through the garden.

I love that garden but none of the official exits land anywhere near my apartment. A few years ago, I found a back door, through the *Musee des Moulages* on the hospital grounds, that let me out near a construction gate right across the street from my building.

I'm just opening that back door when I hear my name and see GIGN, French Special Forces, two officers, huddled like Martians in flak suits, gas masks and sniper rifles, peeking through the construction gate at the wide corner, the entrance to my building and, eight floors above, at the dead coleus drooping from my night table.

Frozen in place, I scan the rooftops and find a squad of dark gray uniforms—and, in case I harbor any last doubts, hear my name one more time from the headset hanging from the blonde officer's right ear. I back instinctively into the doorway, sweating and making twenty-five different plans at the same time.

The bus! They won't be checking the bus on the *Boulevard de la Villette*, that's an answer. Having any sort of answer helps calms the quiver in my legs, brings them back into something like working order.

This is a mistake—it's got to be. If I'd done something to deserve counter-terrorism, I'd remember it, wouldn't I? More importantly, why in hell didn't somebody tip me off? Who do I know at GIGN?

Out through the door and the museum, retracing my steps, back out the far end of the compound, past the *Chapelle* to the *Rue de la Grange aux Belles*. Up toward the roundabout at a regular clip, walking briskly like a Parisian.

Am I thinking of escape? Hell no, I'm just getting pissed. Why hasn't somebody warned me? Why haven't they given me a chance to buy my way out of this?

Oh sure, GIGN makes it look serious but that just raises the price. I know somebody in every department of government and what they cost. Serious things have been undone before.

By the time the bus makes three stops, I know who to talk to—Beltoise, the second man at the *Surete*. He was at our Christmas party just last night.

I *own* him! At least, I should. If I had a middle-class clientele, if I dealt pot or owned a brothel, I could expect a phone call 24 hours in advance of a raid. It's common courtesy!

He'll be at *D'Azur*, of course, charging his dinner to us as usual.

When I arrive, he's tucked into a dim corner. He rises before I can reach him.

"Why is GIGN all around my apartment? You don't warn me?"

His eyes bulge like marbles. "Where's your phone?"

"Phone? Stolen. I got mugged."

He looks *relieved*. "That's why they're not here yet," he mutters and pulls me into the private room in back.

"Nicky, our past history—and the fact that I like you—is why I'll give you a minute's grace before I call you in." He's serious! His face goes cold—not like he doesn't know me, like he's never *seen* me before. "Normal corruption is one thing—but this?"

Normal corruption? Normal corruption is my *specialty*! He's reducing ten thousand years of civilized give-and-take to a catchphrase. Not to mention, it's fed him quite nicely, thank you, over the years.

I look at his face, at the disappointment and condescension there, and realize what a farce it all is. You treat them like princes but the first time you actually need them to put out…they might as well be in insurance.

Faced with this ingratitude, something inside me just gives up.

"Okay," I tell him. "I surrender."

"What?"

"I'll confess, right now. It's the jet ramps, isn't it?"

He looks confused.

"We have this client, a dictator...you know the old joke about, you're not really a country unless you have your own stamps, your own airline and your own beer? Well, he's got commemorative stamps, a brewery, a Mercedes stretch limo and a portrait of himself as Julius Caesar. But he gets embarrassed when his guests have to descend a staircase off the plane.

"There's a staircase on Air Force One' I tell him and he says, 'They could have a ramp if they wanted one.' So when Kumbatta collapsed, we flew a cargo plane in and liberated a couple of jetramps. The guy was so happy, he painted two Cessna's and proclaimed them the national airline. I don't think we *hurt* anybody."

Beltoise settles into the nearest chair, not saying a word.

"That's not it?"

Silence.

"Okay, Napoleon's penis—that was a good deed, I swear."

"*Excusez moi?*"

"It's your Minister of Defence's fault! Not the present Minister, the old one. He had this...thing about Napoleon's penis, that it should be back in France where it belongs."

"It is in France! Napoleon's body is at Les Invalides!"

"The body, sure, but his penis was removed during the autopsy and it's floated around ever since from collector to collector. It's now owned by a urologist, naturally, in Philadelphia."

"Don't be funny."

"It's true. The BBC measured it a few years ago and found it a bit small. Naturally, that outraged the Minister, who insisted the English don't know how to measure. The urologist's price was just *outrageous* so we found a...more generously-sized one around the same age, for a price the Minister could afford. It made him *happy*."

"You found him another penis?"

"Another *old* penis! You think that was easy? How many three-hundred-year-old penises you think are floating around?"

Beltoise stares at me with—I can't tell if it's respect or concern. The odd thing is, to me, this is actually beginning to feel pretty *righteous*. Confession really *is* good for the soul.

"Okay, not the answer. Give me a chance. The eighteen identical one-of-a-kind Moroccan emeralds—"

"No."

"The Van Gogh with the wrong ear missing?"

Beltoise rolls his eyes. "We've never met," he warns, "except for a few state dinners with hundreds of other people I've never met either—but my advice is, you find a quick way out of France now. And don't bother replacing your phone—they'll find you as soon as you do. You understand?"

This is terrifying—Beltoise is a glorified flatfoot with a fancy office. I'm *begging* to be arrested and he's not biting. It's *unnatural*.

"Throw me a bone here," I say. "I don't understand what's happened."

He grimaces. "You know damn well it's the bomb."

"The *BOMB?*"

Of course, I know all about the bomb. I'd arrived back in Paris the day before, just in time for the funerals. Twelve dead, 37 injured, a miracle it wasn't more. A mountain of flowers in plastic sleeves heaped on the rubble, candles arrayed like soldiers in front of the dress shop left somehow intact on the corner.

And a march from the *Place De la Republique* to the *Place de la Nacion*, thousands, orderly and dogged, middle-class families and university students, *Le President* and his rivals, butchers, bakers, artists and computer technicians shuffling through neighborhood streets between broad public squares, solemn and chattering, sombre but fashionable—Paris, formal but somehow intimate. Great buildings and beautiful women dressed in black. Paris is a grand dame, maybe a bit past her prime, but she still knows how to put on a funeral.

'It's an escalation,' they say, the voices that multiply in crowds. Just a few years ago, 'they' were content to shoot up a restaurant or concert hall. Now, somehow, they bring in a bomb the size of a safe to bring down half a block of five-story apartment buildings.

The size of the explosion makes people nervous. Nobody builds a bomb that size to bring down the Rue Breguet. We all sense a grander plan that went awry and the fact that no one claimed responsibility only seems to heighten the tension. You don't even have the consolation of knowing who to be afraid of.

Beltoise, however, has made up his mind.

"It's your shipping certificate!" he yells, no longer caring who hears. "Your company's letterhead! Your *signature* on the bloody thing! You think I will cover for *that*, you're insane!"

I stand frozen for an endless moment, until words I never thought I'd hear myself say come tumbling out of my mouth.

"I didn't do *that*! I'm *innocent*!"

And then, I run.

RUNNING

-You ran?

It's an expression. I know better than to run. I walk at my usual quick pace but not fast enough to attract attention. Okay?

I lose myself in the tangle of back streets, staying off the boulevards, sticking to shorter blocks and parks where I can change direction at will. I stop short in front of angled store windows several times, switch direction several more, take a cab for a short distance and then another to double-back on myself. I'm overdoing it, in truth—if GIGN were really on my tail, they'd just throw on the sirens and take me. Once I'm sure I'm not being followed, I find a thrift shop that's just closing in a church, buy a pair of slacks and a short dark hoodie and wear them out of the store.

-This is tradecraft. Where did you acquire your technique?

Like you don't know. I had a very brief career in—what do you tell strangers at parties? About what you do for a living?

-I don't speak of such things.

We used to call it 'compliance.' I was recruited out of college. They trained me to take in a room or a street, to be invisible when that was useful. Trust no one, calculate the odds, tote up the angles and assume everyone follows their own self-interest.

But they couldn't teach me to be shrewd. I got myself involved in an 'extracurricular' scheme supporting freedom fighters—that is, it became extracurricular once it led to screaming headlines. Next thing I know, I'm getting chewed out in front of a Congressional committee for the exact same things they'd urged us to do in private.

We were thrown out like Big Mac wrappers, three fall guys, small potatoes. A generous severance package—under the table, of course—just go quietly into the night, thank you.

That training comes back to me, now that I'm on the run. Focus! *The bomb! What have I got to do with the fucking bomb?*

I need real information. Somewhere in our files, says Beltoise, is a shipping certificate for a bomb with my signature on it. I can't go home so I almost certainly can't go back to the office. But maybe Harry's apartment is clear.

If this had happened any other time—last week, even!—I could have counted on Harry's counsel, his expertise, his instincts. For fifteen years, he's been there when I needed him.

But that's a huge part of what made this feel like the worst day of my life, even before GIGN's visit. I've no idea if I can count on Harry anymore.

-Explain this please. Who is this Harry and why can't you count on him?

Harry is the majordomo, the ringmaster of our circus, the senior partner in Sandler & Son, affectionately known to staff and select members of the governing elite as Swindler & Son. Everything that isn't about Sara in this story is about Harry.

-And Harry's got problems?

Oh hell no, Harry's got no problems. Harry *is* the problem. Everybody *loves* Harry, *that's* the problem.

And why shouldn't they? Harry makes life a party, a twenty-four-hour Remy Martin and shellfish from the little inlet over *there* and put away your business cards, this isn't some vulgar networking grind, we're here to have *fun!* Remember fun? Harry does.

If you liked the Remy, you must try this cognac—it's Venetian, Dante mentioned it (disparagingly, but he mentioned it) in the *Divine Comedy* and let me introduce you to the Ambassador's wife, she has all the good gossip about the orgies at that other embassy—maybe it was the Czechs but we're not saying. Meanwhile, other groups are discussing 70's film and sex robots and if there's anything else you want to know, the person to speak to is over *there*. The band plays good acoustic jazz, the Argentine tango couple are giving lessons one-on-one on the terrace and the star of the national football club is kicking balls around with enchanted kids and dazzled grownups on the south lawn.

In Paris, of course. That's our home base. It's one of God's jokes—Harry hated the French so, once we'd been thrown out of every other country in Europe, the only place left to go was Paris. Which, of course, he now loves because how can you not love Paris? It's *Paris*, for God's sake.

And the French love Harry. Big gnarly elegant gay Englishman, what's not to love? He ignores their culture, conducts himself like tenth-generation nobility fallen to trade or maybe a good Savile Row tailor, speaks only enough French to be fed and catered to but laughs and charms so naturally, they can't help themselves. Seduction is the French national pastime; they recognize a Master at work.

I was in Mumbai two years ago, picking up a load of Indian cotton. There was a rash of suicides among cotton farmers in Vidarbha and I was able to pick up several farms' entire crop just by paying off the bank loans. I told myself it was a good deed and a good deal. So I'm in the hotel bar at the end of the day chatting up some girl when a man behind me says, "Oh, you work with Harry Sandler? I was in a steeplechase syndicate with him in Ireland once. Took me for £65,000 quid. Most wonderful time I ever had." He bought us both a drink.

Everybody loves Harry; that's what nearly killed us all. As I watched the Iranian commandos lining up on the deck of the ship three hours ago, in their black stocking caps and their Kalashnikovs aimed at our temples, all I could think was, *Everybody loves Harry.*

Fucking goddamn Harry.

THE OFFICE

I returned from Miami on Christmas Eve to the usual turmoil.

-Returned to where?

To Paris. To Sandler & Son, our bombastic office in the *Rive Droite*.

-This Harry, he's your father? Your boss?

Neither. Partner and mentor, maybe. He calls himself Harry Sandler and I'm Nicky Sandler—those are our Paris names. Harry passes me off as the son he had before admitting his sexual nature, since he's not fooling anyone for long.

Harry fell head over heels for our ridiculous office building on the *Boulevard de Sebastopol* the instant he laid eyes on it. Taste? No such thing. The building is a monstrosity, bulging into traffic, squatting like a Lumiere moon rocket just bursting to launch. But attention? Oh yes — you're allowed no other choice. Buff and black, a riot of cornices and pediments, ornamental discs carrying no inscription, heroic statues with no recognizable subject and porthole windows puncturing the bulbous dome, just because. The perfect setting for a business with no legitimate means of support.

"Nicky! Welcome back!"

"Lucien D'Reaux called. His appraiser fingered the Modigliani as a fake."

"Who let him get his own appraiser? Call him back, tell him we found another signature under the frame."

"He knows it's fake!"

"It's a fake Modigliani; tell him it's a *real* Elmyr De Hory."

"It is?"

"No of course it's not but De Hory's the only art forger anyone's heard of—hopefully we can cover the costs. And get someone *good* to fake the signature this time. What else've we got?"

-Can we have a bit more detail, please? Staff names and a capsule of each?

Staff of three that day. It's been bigger a few times and smaller several, usually before bankruptcies or absconding across the border.

Sonya is probably in her sixties but maybe older, built like a pumpkin, dresses like a baroness fallen on hard times, brings incredible quiche to work at least once a week.

Clarice is 33, not pretty but a vamp—sexy, funny, full of confidence and someone who shares nothing about herself, so we're all fascinated by her.

Diamante is Dominican, six-foot-three, speaks four languages, is made of marble, with a juvenile streak a mile wide. As I come in, he's test-flying a drone—*in* the office— and playing some video game on an elaborate setup in the corner. He looks up as I approach and the drone smashes into the wall. I pick it up and throw it on a pile with the others.

"The Swedish cars arrived in Klaipeda six hours early," he reports.

-Swedish cars? What's this?

The Swedes don't have more accidents than anyone else, as far as I know, but their accidents take place just a day's shipping from Lithuania and I happen to know a guy who works the docks at Klaipeda—

-In Lithuania.

Right. So we buy junkers from Sweden, pay maybe €350-500 for them, straighten them out, get them running just enough and ship them to Ivan, who works in Customs—

-In Klaipeda.

Right. Ivan drives the cars home off the lot, one or two at a time like they're his personal property, which saves us the Customs duty.

-No one notices?

Everyone notices—until they get paid, at which point they develop selective glaucoma. Okay?

-I see.

I'm not holding back on you, you have to admit. After this conversation, you could start your own semi-legitimate shipping business—except, what's the point, since I already have one functioning and available for your use, cheap? Have you ever had a better offer?

-Go on.

Ivan sells the cars for €15,000-20,000 apiece and we split the profit. It's not big money but it is reliable and low-risk. The problem in this case is that there was actually good weather in the Baltic, which isn't usual a couple days before Christmas and the ship arrived six hours early.

"What's the problem?" I say. "Just have them wait."

"The port keeps telling them they're next in line to dock," Diamante answers.

"So just have Ivan hustle down and take delivery."

"His wife's giving birth."

"Christ! She's not a team player. Okay, have the ship tell Shore Control they've got malaria on board."

"Malaria? From Sweden?"

"Say they were in Panama last week and the quarantine runs out tomorrow—then buy Ivan's wife a C-section. That shouldn't cost more than half a car, right?"

I climb the steps to my office. Sonya follows me with a phone message—from Rahim.

-Rahim—*Prince* Rahim?

Sure. Prince Rahim, your boss, the man who's waiting outside for all the answers to all the questions. Rahim Suleiman Musafa Hattan, nephew of the King of Wadiirah, fifty miles of land along the Persian Gulf and one insane island in it, 140,000 citizens, twice that in non-citizens on work visas and 11.8% of the world's oil, trusted aide to the King and a prudent, soft-spoken family man. Three wives, to be exact, with two or three kids apiece.

    -You think I don't know this?

I want you to know that *I* know it. And knew it before any of this started.

    -What did Rah-uh, Prince Rahim—want?

The message said he had a watch to sell.

    -He sells items through you? Legitimate items?

Rahim is always legitimate.

    -I never thought otherwise.

Of course not. What you're wondering is, why is he dealing through me?

    -I don't make inquiries about the Prince's business.

That's very wise but you're asking for my story and this is part of it.

Look at it this way—Rahim is a pivotal figure in the most progressive country in the Middle East. Iran and Saudi Arabia both have consulates here even though they won't walk on the same side of the street. *Israel* has a trade bureau, along with Russia, China, Myanmar, the Philippines, Libya, Cuba, Amnesty International, Doctors without Borders and the usual free-market Western crowd. So, naturally, all the other Middle Eastern countries *hate* Wadiirah—while finding it useful for making backdoor deals and diplomatic contacts they don't have to admit to.

All of which puts Rahim in a sensitive spot whenever he has to dispose of something discreetly. Who can you trust when you have so many wealthy and powerful enemies? I'm the essence of transparency. My business depends on discretion. No party to my deals ever knows the other parties and if I called CNN, no one would believe a word I said. You see the advantages?

    -I suppose.

Oh, don't sulk, for Christ's sake. I'm just playing the spy game without the government halo. You should admire my balls, if nothing else.

So apparently, Rahim has a watch—a very nice one, surely—to sell. And the message asks me to keep an eye out for a 'special' race car for him. A Formula One champion—a Schumacher Ferrari, a Senna McLaren—or a Le Mans winner, maybe. Something prestigious, because Lamborghini's and custom Bugatti's are so common in his neighborhood.

-Did you call him back?

No. The message got lost in the shuffle at that point. It became important later on, though.

-I see.

No, you don't—but you will.

HARRY TIME

Just a few minutes later, the call ripples out from Sonya and Clarice at their desks overlooking the street.

"Harry time."

"Harry time."

The whole place springs into action, consolidating piles of paper, shoveling odd magazines and bits of clothing into closets. The place is still a mess but the effort gets everyone fluttering up to Harry speed.

I grab a fat research report off the glossy cabinet by the door and pretend to scan as the elevator creaks to a halt and Harry sweeps in, escorting a severely thin woman in a glittering brocade jacket and a glaze of very expensive makeup.

"...one devotes one's life to service and then the rewards find us—Good day, all!"

"Good day, Harry!"

"So this is our cozy corner, Dame Helena," Harry says, just peeking through the doorcrack. "Now let's off to lunch."

'Oh nooo," says Dame Helena, pushing the door open with a shudder, "it's so wonderfully *colorful*. You must give me the full tour."

"Maybe Dame Helena could help with our research," I say and the game begins. How much of this do you actually need to know?

-Don't hold back. You don't know what details might be crucial. We have to be comfortable with you.

Who's this 'we'? It's just you and me here.

-There are others—

—listening in, you mean...

-who will have to be satisfied at the end of the day.

But what do you mean, 'crucial'? 'Crucial' to what? It's all over now, isnt it?

-Not until the questions are answered. The public record must be satisfied.

If you say so. 'Satisfied' in terms of what, specifically?

`-Specifically, in terms of who takes the`
blame. `Who goes to jail, for example.`

That's a hell of an example. So if you're all satisfied with my story at the end of the day, you'll stand by me?

`-If we're satisfied.`

But you're not going to give me any guidance about the type of story that would satisfy you, are you?

`-We're not in the guidance business.`

No offense but you're not making much of an argument for cooperating. Not much security for anybody other than you, down the line.

`-For you, 'down the line' is distinctly`
`a luxury at this point. You were explaining`
`the game—`

Okay, fine. In the last ten years, it's become clear that, while digital technology has made some aspects of the job easier—for example, researching and identifying customers and merchandise, moving money across borders—it's also made the old con game virtually impossible, that classic con where you drop in on some blueblood, fleece them for all they're worth and just disappear.

Let me be clear: it's still possible to fleece a mark. It's the disappearing part that's become impossible. There are lots more billionaires than there used to be—hell, a million is the new hundred thousand—but they still tend to travel in packs. They use the same stable or the same boat basin or timeshare in Davos or their security guy knows the other guy's security guy. It's just about impossible to stay under the radar for long. You become notorious *so fast* to relations and friends or even Facebook friends.

So the game has transformed. Now the question is: how to do the con *without* disappearing, continuing to operate under the noses of people you've taken—not just staying out of jail, but actually building a stable, predictable business?

To make *that* happen, you need rules. HARRY'S RULES.

"There's no point," Harry told me early on, "trying to devise something so clever that no one will ever figure it out. Someone *always* figures it out eventually—that's why they keep hiring policemen. The trick is to keep them from squawking when they do."

−To keep *what*? To keep your victims from squawking when they realize they've been taken?

Exactly—except, they're not victims. They're our *partners*.

RULE ONE: KNOW YOUR PARTNER. This isn't a 'mark' we're playing; this is an intimate business relationship. We've researched this woman for anywhere from two months to a year. The game is tailored to her—in the end, we'll all be doing this *together*.

However, as Bill Clinton might say, it all hinges on your definition of the word 'this.' Both partners see the same events, that doesn't mean they're seeing them the same way.

"Dame Helena doesn't care for your *collectibles*," Harry squawks, stretched out to his full height, head up and back, literally looking down his nose at me. "All this frenzy over a consumer item."

"It's not a 'consumer item'—the right people would kill for this, if they knew it was available. It's *history*." I see the spark in Dame Helena's eyes. Maybe not greed, I hear Harry's voice in my head reminding me greed is *vulgar*. But desire, maybe? Oh yes, desire, certainly.

"Harry dear," Helena says, "I must know more. It sounds *fascinating*."

RULE TWO: THE PARTNER SHOULD SELF-NOMINATE. They must tell you they want in. This becomes crucial when we get to Rule Five.

"Dame Helena, even the most fabled and influential face challenges—" I begin.

"—the kind you wouldn't want your mother knowing about, much less the people who *matter*," Harry confides, knowing Dame Helena is big on people who matter.

"And sometimes their challenges offer us—and maybe you—opportunity."

The girl from Kazakhstan has arrived.

Harry likes having his hair cut while we woo clients in the office. He's found this cute sex bomb from Kazakhstan, a lithe, raven-haired, five-foot-tall Sophia Loren scale model, poured into a red leather vest and capri slacks (on Christmas, yes). She arrives and Harry will offer the guest the merest possibility of choice, "You don't mind, do you?"

They never say 'no.'

Harry settles into a shortback green-tufted saloon chair with towels forming a mandala on the floor about him, wearing a red silk smoking jacket and looking like a pasha. And if he ever reads that description, he'll buy a hookah, just to heighten the illusion. Treading light is not Harry's way.

The girl from Kazakhstan bats her eyelashes while laying out her scissors and a formidable straight-razor and they banter like lovers, though it's obvious to everyone they never will be.

"The usual?"

"You know what I like."

"Yes, I do. But I'm cutting your hair now. Eyebrows?"

"No, leave them. They scare people. They make me look like I know more than I do." Harry has the eyebrows of a cartoon character zapped by lightning.

All this time, Dame Helena's anticipation is boiling. *Which celebrity has difficulties? Have I heard of them? Do I know them?*

Why is gossip the most indestructible force on Earth? Why is every great magazine in the civilized world gasping for air while the gossip rags keep minting money? Because nothing's more powerful than the desire to know something really bad that isn't happening to us.

"Obviously," I continue as Harry snip-snip-snips, "if you were in that sort of sensitive situation, you'd want it handled behind closed doors."

"Of course!" The woman's oozing sympathy. She's already clicking through a list of famous names. *Are they going bankrupt? Divorcing? Paying off a mistress, a bank or grand jury?*

"Alright, Nicky, she understands, out with it," Harry prods—our concerns are intruding on his haircut.

"I have an item—it's my responsibility to find it the right home. I think you might know the sort of person I need." For now, I'm keeping as far from the question of money as is possible. It *will* come up, of course—but later.

It's Harry's line now. I wait an extra second before stealing a glance in his direction. He's gone dry. I clear my throat twice and he pops back to reality.

"You mean the handbag?" he sneers. His delivery's fine, but we've lost the rhythm and will have to recover.

"It's *not* a handbag!"

"Fine, not a handbag, a Brecken—"

"Birkin? A Birkin Bag?" Dame Helena's got it, oh yes she has, eyes wide as the harvest moon.

`-What's a Birkin bag?`

You're not married, are you?

`-You don't need to know that.`

Well, if you're married to a woman, ask her what a Birkin bag is. Sara explained it to me on our first date. Shoes and bags, she said, are to women as cars are to men. The high-end models are ridiculously overbuilt for any practical purpose, so enthusiasts obsess over hair-splitting differences in function and style.

`-That's absurd. A Bugatti Chiron will go 288. That's thirty miles an hour more than the Veyron and almost a hundred more than most Ferrari's.`

And neither of us would take any of them over 100, assuming we ever had the cash to rent one. I'd live in mortal terror of scratching the stupid thing the first time I took it on the road.

A Birkin Bag is the most expensive, exclusive woman's handbag in the world, and if you think we're scam artists, check *them* out. Hermes admits they limit quantities to maintain scarcity. They're actually handmade *in France*—can you imagine how expensive *that* is?—and named after Jane Birkin.

-I saw a lot of French movies with her.

I saw a lot of her in French movies.

She allegedly sketched the first bag for the chairman of Hermes on the back of an airplane barf bag, so at least they have a way with origin stories. And if you're still scoffing, remember that Bugatti's, like all cars, depreciate. Birkin's don't. Several recently auctioned for over $300,000. They're better investments than gold or Apple stock. Customers pay for special orders, wait years, then receive something completely different from what they ordered—and are expected to be grateful.

Anyway, just the *mention* of a Birkin bag and Dame Helena's eyes are positively glowing. And now I'm going to blow them out of their sockets.

RULE THREE: TELL THEM WHAT THEY WANT TO HEAR.

Years ago, I asked Harry, "How do you keep the partner from suspecting a problem? How can you possibly nail down all the details?"

"You can't," he said. "There's no perfect scam. The trick," he winked, "is telling them a story they desperately *want* to believe. If you're offering them their dearest fantasy on a platter, they ask few questions and barely listen to the answers."

It's like buying a Rembrandt—at this late date, nobody can tell you with certainty that any particular painting is really a Rembrandt. But as long as you have a certification from an art historian *saying* it's a Rembrandt, you can sell it with a clear conscience and an open wallet. As long as we've done our research properly, sized up the client's history and sweet spot, from here on, it's paint-by-numbers.

The room is silent, just the faint scraping of the Khazaki haircut girl sweeping up and gathering her things. As soon as she's out the door, I let Dame Helena have it.

"In this case, we're not discussing a Birkin Bag—we're discussing *the* Birkin Bag. The first one, the one Hermes gave Jane Birkin in exchange for using her name. Number Zero, the first point on the compass, where it all started. So, this item needs to be treated with respect and discretion—"

RULE ONE: KNOW YOUR PARTNER.

"Well, I—you've found the right person, right here. I own six of them already."

Dame Helena's being modest. Our research, long before Harry 'bumped into her' at a charity horse show, says she actually owns *fourteen* Birkin's. We paid off one of her maids to double-check.

Her brood ranges from a white Clemence for a mere €10,000 to a Himalayan Crocodile Palladium for an eye-watering €100,000. Her babies have their own climate-controlled compartment in a walk-in closet the size of my living room on the third floor of her apartment at the *Place Des Vosges*, where Cardinal Richelieu lived a few centuries ago. That's the Richelieu who tried unsuccessfully to kill D'artagnan, *that* Richelieu.

Once Dame Helena's owned a Birkin for four years, whether she's worn it six times or sixty or zero, back it goes to Hermes for 'refreshing', to the tune of €3,000-6,000 apiece.

So, of course, the first thing we have to do now is deny her.

-Deny her?

Sure. Having made sure she wants it bad, now we have to tell her she can't have it.

RULE FOUR: NOTHING REALLY VALUABLE COMES EASY (OR: MAKE THEM EARN IT)

"Oh dear, Dame Helena, I'm so sorry..."

"You see, Nicky, this is what comes of your insensitivity," Harry scolds.

"Nicky, I'm the perfect owner. I've already had 'Birkin arm' surgery! I never go anywhere without—" And she lifts her own personal bag off the chair—not the nicest model, if you ask me—to bolster her case.

"Helena, you'd be the ideal guardian, *if only...*"

Pause now and let the blood rise to her cheeks.

"...if only what?"

"You're too high-profile. People notice everything you wear, everything you carry, everything about your style."

She soaks up this flattery as though it's obvious—it may even be true, within her circle. "Well, I do have a reputation."

"Our foremost responsibility, Helena," Harry intones, sounding like the State Executioner, "is to relieve the owner's...financial distress...without embarrassing her." *Is it Birkin herself? Financial distress?* Every successive level of humiliation only makes the gossip more juicy. "And there's the problem, darling—you're an icon. Every time you leave the house, you'll be calling attention to something we want to hide. Surely you understand."

"I *do*," Dame Helena murmurs so earnestly I fear we've overdone it. I hold my breath for several ticks. "So if I were to buy it, I just couldn't take it outside—or tell anyone I owned it."

"Could you have it under those conditions?"

"I'm *assuming* those conditions," she assures us. "I wouldn't want it otherwise. The poor girl, to have such distress at this point in her life."

"You didn't hear that from me."

"No, of course not. This is a legendary bag. I'll curate it the way it deserves. I won't take 'no'."

My turn: "Dame Helena, sometimes things come to us when a person in distress seeks help from the wrong people, giving trust where it's not deserved. So sometimes we find ourselves trying to honor an agreement long after the original conditions have disintegrated or become distorted. Does that make any sense to you?"

If it does, it's not my fault. I've done my best to cloud any sensible meaning behind seventeen layers of smog and dry ice. All I want her to get out of this dialogue is the sense that something here is not entirely kosher.

–Excuse me?

RULE FIVE: THE PARTNER MUST BE IMPLICATED.

Are we selling the bag off the back of a truck? Did we offer it to someone else who proved indiscreet? Was it lifted from the Hermes museum, if there is such a place?

What's important is, if Dame Helena ever has doubts later, about what she paid or why she can't show the silly thing to anyone, we want her to remember that she sensed something wobbly about the whole transaction from the start—and went ahead anyway.

-You aren't serious, surely. That *works*?

Rich people don't get played just because they have money—they really are the easiest targets. Most have been sheltered and protected all their lives and know it. They're hungry for an adventure that gives the thrill of a dark alley or a steep nosedive—without any real danger, because most of them know damn well they can't handle *real* danger.

Anyway, if we've played this right, Dame Helena knows someone's being taken here—she just doesn't realize it's *her*. And if we get her a little wet with the thought that she's up to something a little bit shady, it gets much harder for her, later on, to call the police or even complain to friends.

The question is, does she realize she's in danger of being taken—or does she think she's part of taking someone else? If it's the first, she'll ask about price. If it's the second, she'll ask about provenance.

"Harry, my darling—" here it comes "—how do I know the bag is what you say it is?"

And that's when I see something I've never seen before. I see Harry fail.

Diamante warned me on the phone the week before. "He's fading in and out. He tried to sell a Ming vase to the Modigliani lady. We don't have *anything* I could pretend is Ming."

And now, it's happening in front of me. Harry's eyes go blank. He's lost the narrative, the melodic line, it's all slipping away.

"Dame Helena, you're right to be cautious," I jump in, a bit too strong but what can else can I do? "Harry said this wasn't for you. You won't hear another word about it."

The problem now isn't just that Harry's failing but that he's *aware* he's failing; the fear distorts his whole being—his body shrivels, face receding. He's groping for words: "Uh…protect…the poor dear…from…uh…"

I lead Dame Helena toward the door. Better to lose the play than have her see through it. Harry moans another of his lines, "Oh, this is just where things stalled with Madame Pellicant—"

"Harry!" I snap. "Names! Jesus!"

Madame Pellicant is our backup pigeon, should Dame Helena fail. She is the second-most-rabid Birkin fanatic in Europe. If things were going well, we could use the rivalry to push up the price with Dame Helena. But only *after* Dame Helena made us an offer, which comes after we've convinced her we've got the real item. With Harry losing the thread, we've jumped the line and these things don't work out of sequence.

"Maybe you should sit down, Harry," I say. "The doctor warned you, when you get dizzy?" I see the offended look in his eye—he's fighting my diagnosis but he still can't remember his lines.

"Sit *down*, Harry," I say again and, this time, he sits, doleful eyes like a basset hound staring at me.

I make excuses to Dame Helena—a missed doctor's appointment, pills that should have been taken. We'll contact her next week to pick up where we left off. She's still interested and I assure her we'll take no action without speaking to her first.

But the damage is done. We've lost the play and Harry knows he's blown it. When I return from packing Dame Helena into a cab, he's gone.

LOST AT HOME

Diamante's got two phones and a tablet wired together on the conference table; he's working the bunch of them at a feverish clip.

"What are you doing?"

"Pokemon Go—we liberated Misty Hannah! A brand-new life of endless possibilities!"

"Great. What's all the machinery?"

"I'm spoofing the GPS." He reads my expression and reverts to English. "You can only catch certain Pokemon from certain locations in the world. I'm not traveling to Australia just because I want a Kangaskhan. So this app tells the GPS I'm in Australia or Antarctica so I can collect more Pokemon."

"There are Pokemon in Antarctica?"

"Sure. There's—"

"We need to find more work for you. But I owe you an apology—you weren't kidding about Harry losing it."

"I wouldn't kid about that," he says, his face growing serious. Diamante and Harry were lovers for almost a year before any of us caught on, Diamante's discretion outweighing Harry's total lack thereof. "Tuesday, he didn't know who he was talking to. I'm not sure he knew who he was."

"How long did it last?"

"Maybe two-three minutes in total but it scared the hell out of me."

"How did this happen? I was gone two weeks."

"He unraveled fast while you were away."

"Should I worry about where he is? I walked the partner out and he's gone."

"It's six o'clock," Diamante shrugs like it's an answer. "You sure you want to see him?" He pulls on his coat, hands me mine and leads me out into the dark afternoon.

The snow whips confetti-like around the trees and swirls in wakes behind the cars on the *Rue Reaumur*. Around the corner through a carpark, on a layer of snow on a metal bench, sits Harry, an old-fashioned bag of peanuts in his hand. Diamante points and sighs and leaves us. I bundle my coat around me and sit alongside my mentor, my friend.

"Whatcha up to, pal?"

"Waiting for the chimes—it's six o'clock," he says, like he was expecting me. The Parish Saint-Nicholas faces us across the street.

"There's no chimes," I say. "There's no clock."

He looks up and crooks a finger. Following it, I see a sundial-shaped window three stories up. Yeah, it's shaped like…more or less, but…

"It's not a clock. Not really."

"Six o'clock. Have you thought about God?" he asks, like the two concepts inevitably follow one another.

"We're not on a first-name basis. What about God?"

"Well, if there is a God, it can't really be a Him or Her, can it? So many different things to different people, that's the powerful thing about God. An idea, an idea so big and central that it leaves room inside—room for multitudes."

I don't remember Harry ever showing an interest in the Almighty—not even the spiritual, as far as I remember. He hands me a peanut. One peanut. Who wants one peanut?

"First there was Old Testament God—good and evil, scary judgment—and hovering right there, just over your shoulder all the time but you never know how to please. Throws you into a fiery pit without a second thought, strikes you blind, orders your father to sacrifice you on the altar and you never know why.

"Then comes Jesus and Mary and forgiveness and compassion but this God sees us as parables, not people. He isn't close by us like the old Father. More forgiving maybe but more distant. Mercy is promised but the guilt just gets worse."

Where is this coming from?

"And then comes the Renaissance and the Industrial Revolution and the Space Age—Science, the New God, the first God in our own image. The Universe as Machine."

"God is dead, you mean?"

"No—God is *Us*. We learn the secrets of the Universe and master them. Split the atom, defy space and time with transcontinental airlines, telecommunications and the

Internet. We mimic God's tricks—they've become tricks, now that we can do them ourselves, the mystery's gone out of them. The Earth was our Mother and your parents are always a resented mystery, aren't they? No more. Now it's girders and silicon and Man worshiping himself. But we resent this God—deep down, we *know* He's us. It's no good trying to please *ourselves*! We crave something bigger—something awesome, something too big to reckon. Restore some of the mystery. Isn't that right, pal?" He's trying to fix his eyes on me but they keep wandering in and out of focus.

O God. I get it now.

"Harry, who am I?"

"You're my new pal. Not on a first-name basis with the Almighty, I like that. Very good."

"But who am I? What's my name, Harry?"

"I'm sorry?" He begins adjusting his scarf, fluffing his hair at the sides over the ears. God, he's pulling all the actor's business he uses when he's forgotten a client's name! No wonder he was spouting—he has no idea, right this moment, who I am. Is he enthralled at something else, something a thousand miles or fifty years distant? Or just blank altogether. One way or the other, he's clearly in the moment. *Lost* in the moment.

And then he rallies. Harry may be lost, but he's still Harry—he can spin without yarn, summoning tapestries from thin air.

"And now we have Money, of course! Darwin turned on his head—*Un*natural Selection! A God we've created, but Godlike only in that it has *no* human characteristics, no moral vulnerabilities, no closeness to us or to anything at all. Godlike in that it's totally self-contained, self-referential. It only cares for success, knows nothing but winning."

I at least get this line of thought, for what it's worth. "And the winners are obvious—"

"Because they have the most money, of course! You don't need to explain the value system—which is good, because you can't. It's self-defined, a perfect logical loop. Of course, the problem is, this God is so much smaller than we are. We have to reduce ourselves continually to stoop to His level. But here's a god, finally, that we can be as contemptuous of as God once was of man."

"Harry, think about what you're saying. It's insane."

"God must evolve to suit the times," he winks and I see in those twinkling eyes that he knows me again.

He gazes at that non-existent clock. "There we are. Six o'clock it is. Feel like a daiquiri?"

Sure, I'll go for a daiquiri—and to watch him, to watch him flicker. Now that he knows who I am, as far as he's concerned, he's totally recovered, as though he never dropped the vase on the floor, as though we both never saw it shatter to a million pieces.

But I did.

The oldest name I know for our trade is 'confidence man'. The words were well-chosen and they pinpoint the problem with Harry. What happens to a confidence man who's lost his grip, his marbles, his ability to think on his feet? What happens to a confidence man once he's lost his confidence?

Nothing good.

REGRETS

-So Harry's unreliable. Wish him a
pleasant retirement and kick him out the
door. But you don't.

Well, like I said, all this craziness erupted in the
middle of surely the worst forty-eight hours of my life. By
the time I'm sure I've shaken off GIGN, approaching Harry's
apartment building early Christmas evening, I really need
his help, in whatever shape I find him.

I circle the apartment from several blocks out, clearing
nearby streets and rooftops before drawing closer. No plain
white vans with antennae at the corners, no plainclothes
with bulging pockets and earpieces, just the normal *flics* on
street patrol and not even many of them. A regular

exhausted Christmas evening. Whatever net GIGN has thrown after me does not yet extend to Harry. Maybe they want me safely put away before tipping him off, before he can start barking to his friends in high places.

Harry's apartment is on the *Avenue George V*, off the *Champs-Elysees*. The building is beyond lavish. Italian marble floors, facsimile medieval wall tapestries, Milanese leather overstuffed couches and a spouting koi pond in the lobby. Maurice the doorman is on our payroll—if anything is awry, his cap will be tilted across his forehead. When, from around the corner, I see a straight-on cap and a smile on his face, I know I'm safe—for the moment.

"Go on up, *monsieur*," he says. "I'm sure you're expected."

I'm not but why argue? You can surprise Harry but you can't embarrass him, even if he's in bed with the cast of 'Aida', including the elephant.

As the elevator doors close, I panic, as though they're closing over me, suffocating and entrapping me. Every nerve is extended to its limit, I have no idea what's waiting when the door opens again. It's not as though I have another choice. Once I danced away from Beltoise, every movement, every decision became potentially life-shattering. But I have to do *something*.

Harry knows everybody in town. And, if he's still lost in the ether, he at least has a laptop with an encrypted VPN connection to our office LAN. I've got to see the shipping certificate with my signature on it; thus far, it's the only tangible piece of reality in this whole crazy story.

The elevator doors open—and there is Sara.

"*You!*" she fumes, stomping around the Moroccan rug (real!) outside Harry's door. "How dare you?"

"Dare I *what?*"

"I can have dinner with Harry Sandler, or whatever his real name is, if I want to."

-And Sara is—

My wife, ex-wife, that's a bit unclear at the moment. Sara's the main reason Christmas Eve was one of the worst days of my life—before this Christmas Day.

On Christmas Eve, I went directly from the airport to our final divorce hearing at her lawyer's offices, in a Beaux Arts chateau just off the *Champs*. It was one of those meetings that remind me that, no matter how much I love Paris, I'll never be Parisian. I wear the clothes, my French is almost serviceable but, unlike a true Parisian, I will never smell great.

Pierre Duillard smells great. I notice the instant I take my seat next to him. If I was across the table with Sara, I wouldn't know this because Pierre's much too tasteful to smell good that far away.

He is, however, a dandy at any distance, a 5'7" whippet in a €5,000 YSL suit that mirrors his silver hair, gleaming teeth that must cost more than the suit and a tie-pin bearing an emerald the size of a pea. A *big* pea.

Pierre is our counsel, one of those hires that pays for itself many times over. He knows everyone who matters at the *Quai D'Orsay*, ministries of government and the High Courts. Pierre knows who to pay, if necessary—but only if. We can't buy the whole fucking government like some of his other clients—it's a godsend to small businesses like ours that Pierre understands that distinction.

"I don't understand why we're here," he rumbles. "We have a settlement on the table. Present it to the judge and let these young people move on with their lives."

He may as well suggest canceling a hurricane. Sara is a force of nature and Nature, at the moment, is against me. Disappointment is a glare lasering across the table.

Sara's *avocate*, Estrella Condido, wears an even darker gray suit under a Louise Brooks haircut. "There is an issue of clarification on an item of shared property."

"Our list of property is comprehensive," oozes Duillard.

"Line 22, 'Loyalty Contingency'? Ambiguous name for such a lot of money."

Duillard sniffs the air, as though something's feathering his nose. "This is a maintenance fund in association with a gift. It will be paid as long as needed."

"A gift!" Sara exclaims like it's an insult. She drums the desk with her ex-smoking hand. Meanwhile, what I notice is, she's—maddeningly—wearing the same dress she wore the day we met.

Is this a needle? Sara's not above wearing the same dress twice in a week, if it's the right dress. But here, it feels like a taunt. She knows I wouldn't forget that dress, that first time.

We met on Bastille Day, at a party at the Anglo-French Amity Association, a club that offers English expats a place to eat blood pudding and complain about French music without traveling far from the mistress's *pied-à-terre*. Harry spends big money for occasional appearances by the English football and rugby teams when they're in town—he puts on a spread and gives away blocks of seats to the games. The club members are wealthy and nostalgic, without any real desire to return home—they're perfect targets for Harry's long game.

I hate these things, so, long ago, I found a balcony to hide in, overlooking a garden which, after several generations of painstaking cultivation, now resembled natural overgrowth.

I'd settled into my seat a moment before Sara slipped through the drapes and plonked down, in unladylike fashion, onto the chair across from me. She was as unhappy as I was to have to share.

"I can't fault you," she recovered. "Boring party."

"There is a gun room. You could shoot your date."

"I don't have a date."

"Husband, whatever."

"I'm here on my own."

"I didn't think they took women as members."

"They *didn't*." She let that sink in.

"Well, congratulations—and my sympathies." She smiled and shot me the eyes for the first time—that frank, challenging gaze that says *Can you keep up?* And makes you want to.

Lust is an electric switch—it's either on or off, there's no middle setting. The switch was thrown with her from the first minute.

"Rooting out misogynists everywhere, that's your hobby?"

"I can't do them *all*, there aren't that many hours in a lifetime."

"So why this place?"

"An old boyfriend is a vice president, simple payback."

"Payback is never simple. Is he here?"

She leaned to the window and pointed him out. I grimaced out of instinct, before controlling myself.

"Yes, I know," she admitted. "I thought I could improve him."

"You see? That's a mistake men don't make. When men pick the wrong woman, it's never in an attempt to *improve* her."

She laughed and the laugh was instantly familiar.

"I know you," I said. "Which was it—Sky News? CNN?"

"Both, if you go back far enough," she waggled a midnight-blue sleeve, as though waving away bad memories. The same midnight-blue sleeve she waggles now, watching our lawyers snipe at each other across Pierre's fancy conference table.

"The gift was intended for the six-month wedding anniversary."

"About a week from now."

"As soon as other arrangements can be made, the fund will end."

"So this is payment for a gift that will not be given."

Sara spits a laugh, louder than strictly necessary. It's amazing how many things she finds to look at that aren't me.

"Why list the gift if you've no intention of offering it?" Condido asks.

"The gift requires maintenance until my client can find another buyer. It is listed as part of the cost to my client of this divorce." Another derisive snort from Sara. "Does Counsel suspect some sinister plot?"

Condido's face is a bland mask but Sara's leaves no doubt she does. She crosses her legs and I realize she's wearing the same *shoes* as our first date!

Kitten heels! I still have no idea what makes them 'kitten heels', but there they are and I remember her swaggering off the Anglo-American Amity balcony wearing them. It was Bastille Day and the Fireman's Ball was in full swing. We were served champagne in plastic cups, danced on an oak table and briefly on the rear trellis of a firetruck.

She asked my opinion of her shoes and I said, "I never pay attention to shoes." She replied, "Then you'll never understand women." And followed up with a monologue on the symbolism of the thing, how shoes could stand for independence or submission, daring or caution, warning or invitation. Or several of those at once. Of course, she refused to attach any specific meaning to the ones she was wearing. She was dazzling, ridiculous and brilliant.

I asked if I could kiss her.

She blew up. "How dare you! I'm trying to teach you something and all you can think of is, 'How can I stick my tongue down your throat'?"

She was really upset and it took me by surprise. Upon a moment's further reflection, it struck me as rank injustice. I'd been in lust for over two hours by then, making conversation and dancing close without a hint of a move. And when did I ask to kiss her? (Notice, by the way: I *asked*!) When she *impressed* me! When she showed me *substance*— hell, an unknown universe!—in objects I would have laughed off five minutes earlier.

And, not to split hairs, but, to me, a kiss is not automatically tongue calisthenics. Sometimes, properly done, it's even romantic. Clearly, however, this wasn't the moment for that discussion.

I just replied, "That's okay, I'll ask again later," as I watched those kitten heels march away from me, up the street.

Now she taps them against the leg of the conference table as her lawyer says, "We see no reason to take anything your client says at face value," and I sink a few inches deeper into my chair. "What is the nature of the gift?"

"It is of no importance; the point is moot." Duillard is laying it on a bit thick, if you ask me.

And then—Sara speaks!

"You only bought it as an excuse for lying to me all the time."

I can't help myself. "I wasn't lying, I was being selective."

"About who and what you are."

"Everything I said was truthful and accurate."

"Leaving gaps the size of the Pacific."

"We were getting to know each other. And then we were in the chapel, feeling no pain and signing documents." Duillard pokes me, not that it does a bit of good.

"If you'd simply been honest—"

"There is nothing simple about being honest."

"You can keep your gift."

"I can't use it."

"Throw it away."

"Can't."

"Pack it in storage for the next girl."

I shake my head. Not possible.

"Why the hell not?"

"It has to be exercised." The room goes quiet, everybody's staring at me and all I can do is sigh and surrender. "It's that blonde filly we saw in Poissy."

Sara sits up straight as an ironing board. She's touched, it's in her eyes, even as she struggles to recover her mask of disillusionment. Here is something she really wanted and would never buy herself. I was right, it's on her face, that and the fact that it's too late, past the point where it could make any difference.

"If you want her," I say, "she's yours. But you have to take over the maintenance and get someone to take care of her when you're out of town."

"You've got somebody taking care of her?"

"Of course I do. I take my responsibilities seriously."

"The sarcasm isn't necessary," Condido protests.

"No sarcasm." I lean across the table. "Pierre told me to include everything in the list. If that's the only problem, we'll take her out."

"It is part of your financial contribution to the marriage," Duillard fumphers. "It should remain on the record."

Like an overwound top, Sara finally comes apart. She grabs the documents from her lawyer, scans them top to bottom and forces a strangled voice. "I don't want gifts from you."

"This is not proper," Duillard complains. "There are procedures—"

"Just take the damn line out," I burst. "Jesus Christ— you're fired!" I grab Duillard's pen, cross out the language in our draft and initial alongside. "Let me have yours," I tell Sara, who hands her paper over. I do the same there.

She sits motionless, staring at the desk.

"Are we done now?" I demand and both lawyers nod yes.

I turn back to Duillard. "You're hired again." The old man nods, all wounded dignity.

"We'll take it to the judge," Condido says. "You needn't stay." Sara's up and out instantly, the shoes clicking hard against the stone floor.

SARA

And now—

-'Now'? Now when?

Now the next evening—Christmas evening—I'm in a hoodie, running from the cops and Sara's yelling at me in the lobby outside Harry's apartment.

"I can have dinner with Harry Sandler, or whatever his real name is, if I want to."

"Fine by me."

"Okay—so where is he?" She points at his door. They had a *date*!

"You've rung the bell?" (she nods) "Out, I guess."

"And you have nothing to do with him being out?"

"I'm *innocent*," I insist, for the second time in living memory. "Actually, I really need to see him."

"He's forgotten?" she sulks, with reason. In the same way I eventually became Harry's spiritual son, Sara and Harry fell instantly into a ridiculous father/daughter besottment.

"He's forgetting plenty these days." I pull his key from my pocket. "Let's find out."

Harry's apartment is the Temple of Gaudiness. What's the most bombastic piece that could go in that corner? Swoops of aluminum flank the fireplace, silk drapes drool across the windows. Why sit in a chair when you can possess a high-back deep-glazed ceramic wonder with Asian lettering no one understands? The lights of the great boulevard glare through the thirteen-foot vaulted glass. The place is exhausting. I head immediately for Harry's study.

The laptop's gone. Is it broken? In the shop? Harry's barely computer-literate. We forced the laptop on him for emergencies. I don't know that he's ever touched it.

Louis XVI would've found Harry's dressing room a bit over-the-top. All I care about is: No wallet, no glasses, no watch. Okay, he's gone for the night. Christmas, he could be making merry with any of a thousand friends—or an equal number of people he's never met before.

Sara exits his bedroom as I arrive.

"Either the bed's not been slept in or he's a hell of a housekeeper," she says.

The bed in Diamante's room is rumpled on one side. And no laptop.

"Best of luck," I nod. "Have to go." But, at the exit, Sara's right behind me, squeezing into the tiny elevator. We stare past each other the whole slow trip down.

Expelled into the lobby, scanning the doorman across the koi pond. Maurice looks relaxed, hat face-forward.

"You know where he is," Sara accuses.

"I really don't."

She's sizing me up, still skeptical. I'm a good liar—I've made a career of it—but I can't convince her when I'm telling her the truth.

"Something's wrong," she says finally. "Is he in trouble?"

"No, he's not in trouble," I say, scanning for the darkest sidestreet as I trot outside, trying to get away from her, away from Harry's building, away from the cops—I can't really catalog all the things I'm running from anymore.

And then a 1959 Cadillac pulls to the curb and Proto Toulouanda aims his pistol directly at my nose. "Come, Nicky, we take a ride, like in the movies."

KIDNAPPED

-Pro—who? Is that a name?

Proto Toulouanda is a one-man conglomerate. Bag man, muscle man, protection peddler, all-around guarantor of reliable outcomes. A very unpleasant person, if he's not working for you at the moment. We know people who know him, but, happily, we've never employed his services nor been the target of them—until now. He wags his pistol toward the open rear door of the car.

"Get inna back. Gimme your phones. My English not bad, so?"

"Not bad, Proto. You want me, yes? Not her."

"Her, too. And gimme your phone."

"I don't have one," I open my jacket. He jumps out and pats down my pockets.

Rene Baudelaire is behind the wheel. Rene is the kind of guy you send with Proto, to make sure Proto remembers the way the boss wants things to turn out. Underworld middle management. At the moment, he's just one more unknown factor. Rene used to work for Gilles De Resnai, a serious boss in the northern suburbs, but they parted company a year ago and nobody knows who he works for now.

"*Bonjour*, Nicky."

"*Bonjour*, Rene."

"And who is this?" Rene eyes Sara up and down.

"Why don't we leave her out of it? I'm sure whoever wants to see me doesn't need to see her."

"She's nice to see."

"She's mute and blind as a bat. No memory, either."

"Then she don't remember going for a ride," Proto says, waggling the gun with a bit more attitude. We slide across the back seat, yards of tufted red leather.

Rene pulls away from the curb. He's sticking to the rear-view mirror, which is no way to drive. Proto's settled into the passenger seat, replacing the gun in its holster.

I'm replaying local politics, trying to figure out who might have sent these two but I can't imagine any scenario that would include Sara. "You guys sure about this? She's not someone I discuss business in front of."

"Nothing to discuss at the moment," Rene says. "Plenty of time." He takes a few turns and we're deep into back streets, the kinds I used earlier to make sure I wasn't followed.

A few twists and turns dump us onto an arterial highway but only for a few stops, then briskly off and through a deeply wooded park—then threading a roundabout and back through the park again. Is it a signal? Do we have company? I lean to pick up the side mirror. Cars flit in and out of view but nobody sticks.

We burst from a claustrophobic neighborhood onto the ring road, a few exits flash by and suddenly we're on our way back. Is Rene trying to confuse us? It might work if we were blindfolded or this wasn't the city we all live in.

Now that I've been a hostage, I can tell you that silence comes natural at first. You don't want to set off your 'hosts'. First, you tell yourself it'll all blow over, that it's just a mistake. Then you realize, of course, it's not a mistake — these guys are pros. You keep your mouth shut anyway, in hopes they'll realize they really wanted to kidnap somebody worth a whole lot more money.

However, twenty minutes later, we're retracing our steps *again*. We haven't picked up a tail, we aren't even trying to shake a theoretical one. At this point, these boys have used up any sense of sinister they once had working for them. If we're not hiding and not going anywhere, what the hell are we doing?

As we cross yet another park, I open my mouth.

"Are we lost?" Sara kicks me but it's time to make at least a little noise. "We've been doing a lot of driving for not getting anywhere."

This is a bit colloquial for Proto and what he doesn't understand makes him mad. He reaches for the shoulder holster but Rene slaps his hand back. Okay, Rene doesn't want us hurt yet. He doesn't even wait an extra second just to scare us. He says nothing but we still don't seem to be going anywhere.

"Really, Rene, you could have just invited me over for drinks," I purr, as pleasantly as I know how. He laughs, not a big yuck, but the tension fades.

"Nicky, life isn't so simple," he sighs and rejoins the highway, as though going nowhere faster shows he's serious. Proto really is serious, but Proto doesn't know any other setting. Is this it? Is Rene accomplishing his mission, just driving us around Paris in his huge American car? If someone's trying to hide me, this isn't the way to low-profile.

And then, like clockwork, I look into oncoming traffic and see exactly what I don't want to see.

"You should get off the highway," I say.

"Stay in your seat," Proto says with practiced menace.

"You're the passenger this time, Nicky," Rene says. "Just relax—"

"A police car just passed, going the other way and he spotted me. If you check your mirror, I'll guarantee he's on the ramp, coming round to this side."

Rene resentfully gives the mirror a glance and sits up all of a sudden. "You're *un prophete*," he admits. "Why's he after you?"

"You don't know? They're all after me. I'm leading the Hit Parade."

"Nicky, don't play with me—" The next exit is coming up quickly on our right.

"No playing, Rene. If you don't get off now, he'll have us all in the Bastille, I promise."

"They don't use the Bastille no more," Proto says and he should know. "You mean La Sante."

"Don't encourage him," Rene says, just as the police car flips on its siren. Rene flinches, hauls the car in front of a honking Renault and onto the exit ramp.

"Alright, what's going on?" he demands. "You got protection?"

"No protection—just trouble. GIGN had my apartment staked out when I got home. They're combing the city for me since early evening."

"Why don't I hear about it?"

"They're keeping it quiet. I mean, they're *really* keeping it quiet."

This disturbs Rene on professional grounds—keeping a dragnet secret from the underworld is a breach of normal corruption.

"Why are you so special?" he demands, corkscrewed in his seat, driving dangerously with his mirrors again. Sara and Proto are staring holes through me.

"They think I smuggled the bomb into Paris."

Proto and Sara actually gasp, like children at the reptile house. "*Merde!*" Rene says, sharply turning a corner and putting his foot down so the Cadillac leaps forward. He eyes me like a *croupier*. "You're a slick guy, Nicky, not a *tueur*. You don't do such a thing."

Sara smacks me on the shoulder. "He's such a liar." The sirens get loud; a couple of extra cop cars have joined the chase. "That's why I'm divorcing him."

"This is the wife?" Rene nods. "Congratulations."

"On the wedding or the divorce?" she asks.

"A man gets kidnapped, his wife should support him," Proto disapproves.

"I'm kidnapped, too. How about him supporting *me*?"

"If he don't support you," Rene says, "we don't pick you up. A woman should show some respect."

"Yeah," Proto says. "What's a wife for?"

"Apparently," Sara says, "to be the other hostage."

Rene makes several quick turns with purpose. Alongside an underpass, then down an alley behind a long line of retail stores. He pulls between huge dumpsters, switches off the lights and waits. He and Proto both pull their guns.

"You're going to fire on the police?" Sara asks and as soon as she says it out loud, the absurdity of the idea is obvious.

"She's not with me, she's not armed or involved," I remind them.

"She's your wife."

"She's divorcing me. We had a final hearing yesterday. And, in case you care, I didn't bring a bomb into Paris either."

"Of course, you didn't do it," Rene says. "I said that."

"Fine, we're agreed I'm not a mass murderer."

"You're not even a *single* murderer," Proto snaps, defending the honor of his profession.

"Well, they think I am—and they're after me."

"I don't get this, Nicky. You've got friends on high."

"Which is good until they decide to bring you in. Then you just have enemies who know your habits."

"You took your time mentioning it."

"I thought you were really kidnapping us, like you were going to stash us someplace. Why are we just wandering, Rene?"

Rene shrugs but the move is an admission. "I'd tell you if I could," he apologizes, his tone all professional courtesy. The sirens get loud for what feels like a very long moment and then fade into the distance.

"I'm just saying, this isn't how things are done, Rene. You're a professional—I wouldn't hire you to do a kidnapping like this."

"You never hired me *once*."

"I've never needed anybody kidnapped. You know you'd be the first..."

"Window-shopper! You lie on the floor." I duck down between the seats and he pulls back out onto the street. Proto turns on the radio and starts hunting news stations.

"I'm just saying you should stash us off the street and check out what I'm telling you. For your own sake. And seriously, let her go, she's not part of this."

The two of them start whispering, which would be more effective if I wasn't lying right behind them.

"We have to."

"Where—?"

"My sister's?"

Seven minutes later, Proto pulls up the driveway of a whitebox veterinary hospital and pushes us in through the back door at gunpoint.

"My apologies, Nicky but now I show you I know how things are done."

Down a hallway of cages, past three dogs, nine cats and a large, cawing crow that keeps pecking at the bars as though he'll eat his way out. Three chairs stand in the office at the end of the hall; Rene waves us in to sit and closes the door behind us. Proto peers in through the door window and then takes a seat in the hallway.

Sara waits just long enough to be sure Proto is comfortable, then jumps to the cabinet against the wall, sorting through multiple shelves filled with bottles and pills with indecipherable labels.

"What are you looking for?"

"An edge," she says. *"You* should be doing this. Why are you letting them imprison us?"

"This isn't such a bad deal for us."

"Excuse me?"

"We're off the street, in a place professional criminals—far more professional than me (she frowns at this)—trust as a hideout. Better than anything I could find myself."

Bottles and boxes come off the shelf, not carefully. Finally, she wags a bottle in the air. "Ketamine."

"What's that?"

"PCP—Special K. A date-rape drug."

"What's it doing *here?*"

"Vets use it for anesthetic." She pulls a paper cup out of the stack on the counter, pulls the cap off the bottle, empties it into the cup and fills it from the water fountain. "Ask Proto if he wants some water."

"Sara, these guys are—"

"I've been held by Columbian rebels and Hezbollah. You want to mansplain me or wait to see if Rene turns you in?"

When I peek through the doorway at an angle, to avoid showing myself to Proto, he's nowhere to be found. I move closer for a wider field of vision. "He's not there." For no particular reason, I try the door handle—and it turns.

"What are you waiting for?" she says but it's too easy.

"Step back from the door, just in case." She does. I take a deep breath and pull it open.

The hallway runs from rear car park to front reception. A young woman answers the phones; otherwise, the place is silent but for barking and cawing. The Cadillac is nowhere to be seen.

We tread up the corridor toward reception, with me carefully checking each intervening office—until Sara blows right past me.

"Rene around?" she asks the receptionist—is this Proto's sister? There's no resemblance but a female version of Proto is too grisly to imagine. "Or Proto?"

The front door buzzes loudly behind her. "*Joyeux Noël!*" the receptionist says, handing Sara back her cellphone. "The door will lock behind you."

Out in the street, the wind tosses filtering lines of snow off the edges of nearby warehouses, dark boxes cut from the starry sky. The road is narrow and empty, alternating pockets of streetlight glare and deep shadow but the drum and hiss in the distance speaks of nearby highways. I thought I knew roughly where we were but maybe I was conflating this neighborhood with one we drove through ten minutes ago or twenty or thirty. This far outside Paris, we might be anywhere.

I march away, not worrying about direction. Our first job is to put distance between us and the vet hospital, in case Rene changes his mind and calls the police.

Four blocks away, the warehouses thin out, I can see open land ahead and a few main roads intersecting. Sara's watching me, noting the things I pay attention to and the decisions I make. She did the same thing when we started dating.

"Go home now and stay there," I tell her. "If anybody asks, you ran into me at Harry's, Rene kidnapped us but didn't take us anywhere, dropped us off at the vet hospital and I took off. You don't know why they dropped us off or where I've gone. Don't change anything that happened, just leave out knowing anything about my situation."

"What the hell just happened?" she demands, as though a dam is breaking. "They just decided to stop kidnapping us?"

"That was not a kidnapping. A kidnapping has demands, someone to pay off, a goal. These guys drove around like tourists." A siren wails just up the road—I pull her into a doorway, holding her close for a moment and the car passes. The feeling between us is familiar and doesn't pass so quickly. "Just go home. Be glad to be rid of me. If the police don't come, get on with your life."

We reach an incongruous gingerbread house, a farmhouse for a hundred years, surely, until the land was sold for window frames, propane tanks and a ticket to someplace far away and cheaper. Twenty yards of railroad track cut through the street and then vanish. Once, not long ago, those tracks went somewhere. A roundabout sits on the other side of the house, a four-lane road cutting through what must have been the farm, with just a few cars whistling by.

Maybe I can get a cab.

Moment of truth: can I risk a cab? Is my face all over the news? Have they named me to the public? More importantly, who are *they*? Who's fingered me for something I didn't do? Who's *behind* all this?

Stomach churning, regret burning my cheeks, I think maybe I know.

THE PARTY

Harry must have everyone around Christmas Eve. It is his holiday, D'Azur is his cathedral and—

-Wait! This is a memory again? We're back to Christmas Eve?

I told you—everything happened all at once. I returned to Paris Christmas Eve, went directly to the divorce hearing, then back to the office, where I found out Harry was running on three cylinders and, that evening, which is what I'm talking about now, we had our Christmas Party.

-And then?

Well, once I tell you about the party and the meeting that came out of it, you'll be caught up through Christmas evening, when I got mugged and stumbled onto GIGN watching my windows.

-From here on, try to keep it clear, please.

I'll try for your sake but it sure wasn't clear when it was happening. My head was spinning.

-(under his breath) *Your* head—

Anyway, like I said, it's Christmas Eve and Christmas Eve is Harry's holiday, D'Azur—the *nouveau cuisine* restaurant down the block—is his cathedral and our staff are his choir. No delicacy will be passed up, no course rushed or skipped, everyone must have a wonderful time or he will know why not.

This year's festivities are notable for two unusual occurrences, events that seemed peripheral at the time but stick out now like the Hazmat suit in the dumpster.

The Christmas Party participants list has grown over ten years to include the Chief of Police, the Mayor, the Prime Minister and *Le President* (at different times, to avoid each other), ambassadors, film actors, the occasional opera star and a duo Harry chatted up on the Metro, who now perch happily in the corner doing a very good imitation of Django Reinhardt and Stephane Grappelli.

Anybody Harry knows may have been invited and any smart human being, invited to a Harry party, shows up; in this case, an Assistant Minister of Something is fuming in the vestibule because Harry *hadn't* invited him, but, in seconds, he and his mistress (maybe she's even his *wife!*) are sucked into the festivities and assured it was all a mistake. "Someday soon, in the way of things, he won't be an Assistant anymore," Harry winks.

We raise our glasses. "What do we *really* celebrate every Christmas?" I ask.

"Being alive," Harry answers. "Being in this place, able to pay the bill—and sometimes, not actually having to pay it."

Harry set up a charge for us at D'azur in the early days and, whenever they were about to dump us for non-payment, he would charm another restaurant critic into dinner there, followed by an ecstatic review. Our second December 24th extravaganza coincided with a visit from a Michelin writer high on ecstasy; Harry thanked D'azur loudly for 'the fantastic Christmas Party they've thrown for us.' After the Michelin star appeared in the window, they stopped pushing us for payment.

On this night, each platter brought by the waiters prompts cries of approval and gusts of applause. Yves, the maitre d', well into the spirit of the evening, cries, "You like *that*? I have something *better!*" and sends something better until they've run through the menu and are making shit up in the kitchen.

After an hour, the table is a wreckage of canapes, squid, sausage, anchovies and eggs and pimentos and eel and prawns and scallops and avocados, melon and berries, three kinds of wild rice, pasta, roasted potatoes, boar, lamb, venison, buffalo and more. That's what's still left after eating and who can take it all in? Entrees are superfluous but several appear, just in case, followed by speculative desserts and uncounted bottles of brandy.

Meanwhile, the crowd along the wall is debating Art and cooking, the IMF rape of Greece, the best old comic books that now suck, the insane cost of apartments and the best wine to drink with the wine we've already drunk. The *Hot Club de France* duo is sprinting through an amazing 'Honeysuckle Rose' and all the world's disappointments are distant and irrelevant, like God.

And I cast my eyes around and realize, I could never do this. I never would and never could collect such an assemblage of people, bring them all together in such a way that the artists become obliging and the politicians almost human. I would never know how to have this much fun on my own. That's what I owe Harry.

And then, around the fifth round, Millard Hastings joins the celebration.

-Hastings? The State Department spokesperson?

That was years ago. Now Vice President of some management consulting firm—a management consulting firm no one heard of five years ago (although they insist they were founded in 1948), somehow with offices in fifty major cities and billions in assets. We've maintained a steady but low-key business with him for several years, arranging shipments to and from Beirut, Dubai, Basra, Singapore, Guam, Panama and other locations. Generic containers shuttling from one gigantic warehouse complex to another, the whole interlocking machinery controlled by him, ownership tunneling through multiple shell corporations.

-So he's a client.

Sure, if Joe's Hardware can call Amazon a client. It's bizarre to see him at the Christmas party. My impression was he wanted to be not just a silent partner but an invisible one. I can't recall him ever showing up at any of our shindigs before, yet here he is.

"Which wine?" Harry asks, always the host.

"What's the difference?" Hastings says, waving the red flag in front of the bull.

"Excuse me?" Harry blanches. "Have you never noticed the red wine glass is larger than the white?"

Hastings just stares. "I assumed there were just two sizes—"

"Absolutely not. The choice is canonical. Red wine glasses are larger because red wine is superior to white."

Clarice groans—she spends the week listening to Harry spout—which only makes him grin the wider. His cheeks bunch up around the ears, his teeth bulge so prominently you think he's going to take a bite out of someone's forehead.

The maitre'd appears magically—I'd swear he wasn't in sight a moment ago—and Harry challenges, "Yves, why is a red wine glass larger than the white?"

"Reds are bolder wines," Yves explains, without a suggestion of a set-up. "The bouquet and the flavors require more space to reach their full potential."

Hastings looks unimpressed, even (!) uninterested. He sips at his drink (red) and keeps eyeing me.

"What about *this*?" Sonya challenges, pushing her fluted champagne glass in front of Harry. "Why is *this* different?"

"Well, that…" Harry gulps a breath and we await a lengthy pronouncement, "uh, that is, as they say, there's never…ahh…just one way to…these things…"

"What things?" Sonya asks. Diamante elbows her but too late. The panic creeps across Harry's face. The conversation falters and then picks up again, a bit too loud this time. The entire staff turn their attention to anything and everything other than Harry. He's shaken, white as the tablecloth. He's faltered in front of witnesses.

"The grooves channel the bubbles," I say loudly. All he has to do is tell me I'm wrong and he's back in the conversation.

But he can't do it. Harry won't be placated or rescued, he wants to *recover*, to rebound like he always has. He remembers quite clearly who he's always been. That man, unfortunately, isn't available at the moment.

And then, casting about, Harry's eyes open wide and a smile big as the Western sky bursts across his face. He shoots out of his chair, loping toward the bar like an Olympic sprinter.

"Darling!" he erupts, arms wide open as he sweeps over…to Sara, who's just entered the room and recoils, seeing us against the far wall, her expression as stricken as Harry's was a few moments ago. As stricken as my expression is, seeing her.

Our group hasn't just stopped talking—I swear they've ceased to breathe. Both Hastings and the Chief of Police know about my divorce. The Chief, to his credit, just looks embarrassed. Hastings looks like a lion stumbling on a wildebeest carcass.

Harry grasps Sara's arm and sweeps her over to the party. "We've been waiting for you, darling, you've just missed the most lovely wine."

"Harry, I don't—"

Sara's totally conflicted but won't—can't—contradict him, though clearly she would prefer to be anywhere else in the world.

"Nicky my boy, make way for your lovely bride."

I pull out a chair and, graciously, she takes it, glaring as though this is a plot of mine. Our group bursts into boisterous, competing discussions, each trying to bury the moment before it can breathe.

"He doesn't know," I stage-whisper at Sara as soon as Harry turns away.

"Of course he does! You are *pathetic*! You'd say—" Her voice cuts through the chatter and the volume drops by half, the whole group (Harry included) staring at us for an incredibly uncomfortable moment before picking up where they left off.

"Remember the story you told me about your father? At the end, when he was...living in the moment?"

That penetrates. Sara's father was a major force in NATO foreign aid, orchestrating relief efforts, food here, construction equipment there, developing new sources of funding as the old ones dried up. His dementia was almost impossible to keep private but Sara knew if it made the papers, it would be front-page news (she was right about that) and that, once he saw it in print, his resistance would collapse. Right again—the man retreated to a bare southern bedroom, watching the light change, ignoring anything that required more knowledge than could be found in a look.

She stares at Harry now and returns to me several times, lingering in suspicion. It's only when she soaks up the terrified looks on staff faces, realizes how they're ignoring the blank spots in his conversation, maneuvering to protect his dignity, that her anger transforms to pain. She may not believe me but she can't help but believe *them*.

"How?" she hisses. "I just spoke to him —"

"Three months ago," I fill in. "I spoke to him two *weeks* ago and there was no problem then, either. We're trying to get him to see a doctor but he's not real cooperative."

"So what," she asks, glancing around guiltily, "do we do now?"

All I can think to say is, "Eat."

The table conversation—the group now comprising Hastings, the Trade Minister, the aforementioned Beltoise of the *Surete* and me—has turned to the question of how to ship artwork that might not be too legitimate across borders.

**-Which isn't legitimate—the artwork or
the shipping across borders?**

For our purposes, it doesn't matter. It's the same game
as with Dame Helena—HARRY'S RULES at work—a
pleasant, supposedly theoretical discussion of how to get
around their security precautions, so that, if the subject ever
arises again, they will guiltily remember the Christmas Eve
they taught us how.

At the moment, however, it's my game—Harry lingers
on the periphery, timid and reticent, knowing he should
contribute but not trusting himself to.

"What about handmade furniture?" I suggest. "Build
the pictures into the rear wall of an armoire. Crate the
armoire, put the special pieces in the middle of a shipment
of twenty, so the X-ray man gets bored, randomly tests a few
and lets the rest sail through."

"I don't know," Harry finally offers. "How do you
ensure they pick the wrong pieces to X-ray?"

"Half the world's nuclear radiation detector operators
can't read the damn screen," Hastings pitches in, "and
they're the cream of the crop. If your painting isn't flashing
neon, they're not going to pick it up."

Beltoise, the *Surete* man, frowns at this. "It makes no sense to be clever," he says. "Everything clever has been done. We have seen it all before and we will catch you."

"Okay, then how about this?" I say. "We take the paintings out of the fancy frames, roll them in rubber bands, throw them in the back of a cheap hatchback with a couple of boxes of books and send them across the border in a Fiat 500 with Sondra's idiot cousin and his bombshell girlfriend."

Beltoise smiles. "That might work," he admits.

"It can't be that simple," says Hastings.

"Simple is the *only* thing that works consistently," I tell him. I'm preening a bit but maybe it'll stir us up some business. At least it might give him something to remember other than Harry's collapse. "Let's say I bribe a foreign minister in a foreign country because I want to export a few zebras. The Foreign Minister has a big house and a Mercedes and two mistresses, he doesn't *need* my $50,000. Meanwhile, there's a city full of guys who resent him and want his job, because he's Foreign Minister and they want their *own* $50,000 bribes. So they watch his every move until eventually, they catch him and charge him with $370,000 in bribes last year, which seems like a lot of money. He ends up in jail and I end up on a blacklist as a friend of his and can't get a zebra for years or until that government passes out of office.

"So in reality, it's much better if I just bribe Menuhan, my laundress's cousin's friend on the loading dock. I give him a thousand bucks, which is more money than he's ever seen in his life. He gives $150 to the inspector, walks him past the container with the zebras and drives them home, two at a time, in his bakery van. Nobody stops him even if the van whinnies now and then, because everyone knows Menuhan, he's a nice guy with a wife and six kids to feed. The $850 left after bribing the inspector buys school clothes and pots and pans and a new roof on the house and it's gone so fast it's like he never had it. And everyone feels good that Menuhan had a profitable day at work because all he owns is dirt and no one envies him."

"As I said, that might work," Beltoise nods with a smile. I bet he knows a lot of Menuhans.

Hastings takes all this in, nursing a single malt with his scungili. When he gets up to go, he leans into my ear and says, "When can I drop by tomorrow?"

"Tomorrow's Christmas—"

"What better day for a private chat, just the two of us? You don't have any—" he nods, confused, at Sara alongside me. "I'd heard you didn't have family obligations anymore."

"I don't," I say, hearing the bells toll. "One o'clock? Two?"

"One sounds good," he says and he's gone, leaving me with the glare on Sara's face.

"You really didn't think I'd figure out the truth about you?" she says. "This is what I do for a living, finding *facts*. Maybe you didn't lie to me directly but you didn't trust me, you didn't share with me. You never treated me like a partner."

This is her at her best. Offended personally, naked and raw, no mask, no sarcasm, no lawyers. And me with no defense, just the truth.

"I never felt I was lying to you—I thought you saw through me from the beginning. I figured you had me pegged from the first instant."

"I did," she says, "but you made me reconsider." And I know we're thinking of the same moment.

It was our second date. We'd spent 10 hours wandering Paris, just going whichever way looked interesting. I was convinced I was following *her*. At some point, I realized she was monitoring me the whole time—which passersby did I size up (almost everyone), which shops did I stop at—and when we'd approach a corner, which direction did I want to turn.

I stopped dead. "You're sizing me up," I complained. "This isn't a date, it's another interview."

She actually looked like I'd caught her out. "I'm trying to understand what I feel about you," she said. "When I yelled at you the other night—because you wanted to kiss me—it felt really liberating. With a man, I usually feel my only choice is either to be 'nice' or knee him. When I told you off, I assumed it was over. You just shrugged."

I shrugged again. "I know I like you. If you don't like me back, that's up to you. Maybe you've got a point, who knows?"

"I do like you. I feel like I get to be myself around you. I just don't understand it—you're really not my type at all."

And, as soon as she said it, I heard a voice inside my head saying, *How can I not be your type if you won't tell me who you want me to be?*

A wave of embarrassment passed over me, like I'd caught myself out, like I'd overheard something I wasn't meant to hear. I had to replay the line several times in my head before I grudgingly came to accept it.

So much of my success, over the years, had come from making myself into whatever I thought my date or client or bank manager was looking for. If it was just about making a buck, I'd have come to peace with it, but clearly this went deeper and the thought made me squirm a bit. It sparked something inside me, a disagreeable impulse.

"So what *is* your type?" I demanded.

"I want a *warrior*," she answered and that lit the fuse.

"Bullshit," I said. "The problem with warriors is, they're only good in a war." I said it and *meant* it. There—I'd said something I *meant*! "Otherwise, they're rude, paranoid, overly aggressive, driving like idiots and getting into stupid fights with random bystanders. Women always think they want danger and then can't understand how they ended up with such assholes."

It was pure reaction, striking back without considering the consequences. When I looked over, suddenly concerned that I'd insulted her, she had a smile on her face. "I'll consider that," she said, and I could see she meant it. Which was just one more thing to admire about her.

And so now, six months later—at the Party on Christmas Eve—

-Thank you.

—sitting together in D'azur, the memory of that moment summons a last defense out of me.

"You know where you go wrong?" I tell her. "You ferret out somebody's weak spot and decide that's the most important, insightful thing you know about them. And, politicians and generals included, people aren't their worst impulses any more than their best."

She gives me that same once-over, like she's seeing me again for the first time.

"Did you really buy me a horse?"

"You want to see? I'll take you by the stable."

"No, I don't want to see him. Sell him."

"Her."

"Fine. Sell her. You should be able to do that."

NEW BUSINESS

And the next morning, Christmas Day, having slept very little and poorly at that, I stumble into the office for our one o'clock meeting.

So: Return to Paris Christmas Eve. Divorce hearing, Harry's bonkers, Christmas party, not much sleep, now we have a meeting. Got it?

-Got it.

And right after the meeting, I will stumble onto the street, get mugged and find GIGN all around my apartment. Okay?

-I don't need everything spelled out, thank you.

I must have gotten the wrong impression somewhere. Anyway, Diamante hands me strong coffee as I exit the elevator—I don't care what Hastings says, I don't take meetings with spooks without a witness. And the way the elevator descends as soon as I exit and returns in seconds with Hastings and a crew of four only confirms my suspicions.

"I was going to use the chairs by the fire but I guess it's the conference room," I say, waving them in.

"You brought your support," Hastings answers. "I brought mine."

Some of his are armed, I note, bulges under the armpits they don't bother to disguise.

"This is Dieter Miller," Hastings says, "and this is Mr. Woczynski," not bothering to introduce the other two and what I hear is *No point giving you more names as they'd all be fake anyway.*

Mr. Woczynski is 5"6", as broad as he is tall, with a face as indebted to wolves as human ancestors. Dieter is a killer, a professional. I've seen those dead eyes before. If this was your platoon leader, you'd knife him the first time you had him alone, knowing he'd otherwise lead you to slaughter without a second thought.

The whole group share the security eye-flick, that roving analytic eye that weighs every corner, window and doorway, as a means of attack or defense.

"Dieter and I share a professional—"

"We're in compliance," Dieter says, cutting him off short in a vivid Texas accent. Of course it is. "We have a proposition and Millard here says you'll be interested."

"'Compliance'," I muse.

"Sure," Dieter says. "You know all about that."

"I've heard the term—"

"You did your time," he cuts me off. "I know your history. You shouldn't have any problems."

I always assumed Hastings knew my background, that I was a spook for a short while, before he started working with us. Guys like him appreciate that, it saves having to explain a lot of things out loud. As Ronald Reagan declared, you can't blame someone for what they haven't said.

But Hastings never actually mentioned it. Dieter has made a point of it, in the first ten seconds of our acquaintance.

"You locate some items for us and get paid a lot of money," Dieter says. "No need to spell things out." This has been the basis of our business with Hastings all along, but suddenly I want to know more.

"*Why* don't we spell things out?"

"Why should we?" Dieter snaps. "We all know the score."

That's it. Dieter's finished. No discussion. The man talks like he's got something on everyone in the room. Maybe he's got something on Hastings.

-Why do you say that?

Hastings is generally full of stories, chipper and distant all at once. Today, he's an elongated lizard, the eyes and tongue moving while everything else remains frozen, watchful and anxious. And these are *his* people at *his* meeting!

Dieter drops a corporate ID on the table and I begin to understand. Laser-engraved logo, barcode ID number and a hologram of his face that, on close examination, is too small for fine detail. All I need, really, to understand the bigger picture is the company name, Parker Meridien.

Parker Meridien is a beast, a stench from one end of the planet to the other. They guard foreign ministers and corporate chairpersons, build bridges, drones and telemetry systems and manage food service for military bases. Underneath all that, they run spies, of the corporate, military and cyber variety.

So that explains Dieter but not Mr. Woczynski, who seems to be sizing us up for dinner. Dinner, as in, us on a plate with a cream sauce.

"What if I still want to talk about the score?" I say, trying to feel out the pecking order here, to locate the source of Hastings' discomfort.

"You get money instead of talk!" Dieter says, in a voice hungry for violence.

"Money!" echoes Mr. Woczynski, like the drunk who suddenly realizes he's supposed to be part of the conversation.

"You said he was alright," Dieter confronts Hastings, who shrinks a bit in his chair.

"Nicky, where's your enthusiasm?" Hastings asks, without any of his own. "You have concerns?"

Yeah, I've got concerns. Hastings is no choir boy and he's nervous, so I am too. And if I'm going to back out of this, I can only do it *before* I've heard the details.

"My question is, what do you need *us* for? We're shippers. You and Dieter don't need a shipper. You're already inside the gravy train."

"What's dis Gravy Train?" Woczynski growls.

I glance at Dieter. Does he want to explain? No—he wants to hear it from me.

"All I know is professional gossip. First, it's the charter airlines, supposedly independent businesses that everyone assumes are Pentagon fronts. Parker Meridien should get you unlimited access to them. And for those special packages, there's the shadow planes that don't officially go anywhere at all."

"'Shadow' plane?" Woczynski again. All eyes on me for the answer.

"Military Transport. They're Pentagon, too, and official—but without flight plans, no log of arrivals or departures, no record whatever of comings and goings. They used to be the rendition planes. The 'Space-A', space-available flights. With friends like that, why do you need *us*?"

This provokes a rustling among the eye-flick crowd. Hastings rushes to suture the damage.

"Look, Nicky, you're right—there's plenty of business out there, but it's stupid—*retail*! It's a wide-open highway and everyone's running little station wagons. We want to open a trucking line. Short-term but big-mouth. We have a chance at a truly historic haul, over a limited time period, done and done." He smiles, an almost-convincing replica of his ebullient self. "Besides, you're not doing the shipping, just a very specific type of procurement."

"We deliver to Mr. Woczynski," Dieter says. "He pays us in some rare stuff we want in exchange. You find the stuff—you know the players and how to convince them—he pays for it, you deliver it to us. Simple."

"Now, there is a time window, the whole thing needs to be done quickly," Hastings clarifies. "And no ripples. Everything has to be discreet, everyone has to be satisfied after purchase. I've assured Dieter and Mr. Woczynski that that's your stock in trade."

-So do you have any sense at this point
of what they are selling to Mr. Woczinski?

The only thing I know so far is that they aren't telling me and that I'm not supposed to ask. Frankly, there's nothing new in that—it's how we work with lots of people, including Hastings—but this time, Hastings seems really tetchy about it and Dieter wants to cut off all discussion. So that is what concerns me.

I hold my tongue for several seconds and, as often happens, am rewarded with a bit more detail. "Mr. Woczynski's payments come from several accounts in Cyprus," Hastings continues. "You will have direct computer access to those accounts at all times. Dieter will provide you with a list of items he and his partners want. You'll pull money from the accounts, acquire the items and deliver them. It's that simple."

This is getting *less* simple by the moment. The Cyprus address confirms what I'd already suspected—Woczynski's connections are Russian Mob or Russian oligarchs or just people very very very close to the Kremlin. The kind of people who expect you to twist yourself into a pretzel and eat a hand grenade so that things stay simple for them.

"So, on paper," I say, clarifying—fuck what Dieter wants, "we are agents for Mr. Woczynski? Or for Dieter and partners? Who's paying us to deliver the items from the list?"

"Since none of this will ever become public, choose whichever answer you prefer."

"And we're not concerned why Mr. Woczynski is feeling grateful?"

"Correct. Your job is simply to facilitate his gratitude. You will take a ten per cent commission each time he makes a deposit."

"Ten per cent of?"

"The total amount of the deposit."

Wow.

"And, of course, you'll incur expenses finding and shipping the purchases. Reimburse yourself for those as well. There will be no accounting of these details."

Wow wow.

"And for shipping," Dieter adds, "you can use Military Transport, since you already know how it works."

He drops five ID badges on the table, with Parker Meridien ID and hologram, each with a different cover name. He adds five sets of passports—US, UK, Australia, Canada, New Zealand—names matching the corporate ID's. "Slip a passport photo into the slot," he shows me how the slot closes seamlessly so the picture looks laminated in place. "Book transport as necessary using these ID numbers. Here is a list of friendly staff sergeants on duty each day at

Military Transport bases around Europe and the territory they typically fly. If they have any questions, have them call the number on the card and you'll be verified. Make sure they call *this* number."

"And in case anything goes South—"

Dieter shrugs. "We'll do an investigation and discover our temporary ID system is all fouled up. Someone will probably get fired. But you're being paid extremely well to make sure nothing goes South."

"Every once in a while," Hastings purrs, "you may find the amount of money deposited may be in excess of what's necessary to secure the items and delivery. In which case, the funds go into your discretionary fund."

Meaning, our pockets. Jesus!

-So what do you understand at this point?

Well, it's pretty obvious—they're selling contraband to Woczynski, whose money isn't strictly all that good. They want us to launder his money, convert it into items that will retain their value—or that they can turn over for cash without difficulty—and get those items to them without customs or tax issues.

This is a slush fund of unbelievable proportions and we're being offered 10% plus whatever spills off the spoon. Money laundering on a massive scale. Worldly success beyond any dreams I've ever had.

-Congratulations.

Go fuck yourself. I'm terrified.

-Isn't this your business?

RULE SIX: DON'T GET PIGGY. We're a boutique operation by *design*. Big success means big visibility and when you get too visible, someone gets resentful and takes you down. And right now, I'm watching us morph into a fifty-story jewel-encrusted hog. A fifty-story hog it's too late to back out of.

"You're going to tell us where to find your new toys?" I ask, trying to narrow down the guidelines. "Or is that our job?"

"Most of the time, we'll tell you. There may be times where you'll have to do some research—which you can charge for."

"I assume the requests will be very specific, which is why the items are so valuable."

"Correct."

"Are they already for sale?"

"Sometimes. Sometimes they're just out there somewhere."

"And if the owner doesn't want to sell? Do you furnish us with an alternative?"

"Sometimes," Dieter says. "Most of the time, we want what we want." Which means, *Steal it if you have to, not our problem.* Wonderful.

"Anything in particular you want right now?" I'm just asking this to buy time to think, to find a loophole. I'm not finding any.

Dieter leans back now. *This* conversation, he likes. "A Porsche 917—racing car from the Seventies."

"917K, 917 *Langheck*, 917-10 Spyder, 917-30? 12 or 16-cylinder?"

"There are no 16-cylinders."

"There's one in a private collection—in Estonia at the moment but I could have it in Paris next Friday."

"You know your 917's."

"I have a couple of standing orders, for particular models, if they become available within a price range. As far as I can see, you don't have a price range."

"I want a Le Mans winner." Rahim first and now Dieter. Except Dieter will actually pay what it costs. And why not? When you have more money than God, of course, you'd want a Le Mans winner.

"They're in the Porsche museum," Dieter continues. "So if you want to show—"

"Actually, they're not."

"Not what?"

"The 1971 winner is in the Porsche museum, that's true. But the 1970 'winner' in the museum is actually chassis 001, which was a test car only, never raced. The real 1970 winner is chassis 023, which is in private hands with a historically incorrect paint job."

"Why haven't I read that?"

"I have the documents from *Automobile Club de l'Ouest*, who sanction Le Mans, citing the chassis number. I have the pictures we took at the Porsche museum, showing they have a substitute."

Dieter leans over the table. His smile is chilling. "Just make *sure* I get the winner," he says.

CROSS PURPOSES

-And so, because of the meeting, you decide Hastings and friends framed you for the bombing? Does that make sense?

Does *anything* make sense? Maybe they weren't framing me, maybe some enemy of theirs is trying to get at them through me, I don't know. All I know is, they're scary dudes into scarier shit than even I am used to and I leave that meeting, get mugged and find GIGN on my doorstep, all in the span of an hour. If nothing else, the timing is highly suspicious. Could all that really be a coincidence?

-Einstein said 'Coincidence is God's way of remaining anonymous.'

Yeah and Yogi Berra said, "That's too coincidental to be a coincidence."

And that's how I end up in the cold, three blocks from the veterinary hospital with Sara, eyeing the roundabouts and sizing up the taxicabs and trying to figure out the next step—with Hastings and friends a really bad chill up my spine that won't go away.

"Do you think somebody kidnapped Harry?" Sara asks.

"If they kidnapped him, they'd be calling me for money." I reach into my pocket and realize, "No, they can't," and I tell her about the mugging, my missing phone.

"You think they mugged you to get your phone? So you wouldn't interfere?"

"You mean, someone *else*? Someone kidnapped Harry and somebody else kidnapped us to keep us from looking for Harry? Somebody who doesn't know I can't go to the police because they think I exploded the Rue Breguet?"

"It sounded better a minute ago," she admits. "You *didn't* make that up about the bomb?"

"*Surete* have my signature on the shipping certificate. Jacques Beltoise told me."

"He's a moron. And a misogynist."

"He's a French bureaucrat. And a man with zero imagination, so he didn't make it up. Next."

I scan the horizon, roads running off in every direction, none of them taking me anywhere safe. So much for the long view.

When I turn back, Sara's posed with hands on hips like Supergirl, sizing me up. "This is stupid," she says. "You didn't bring a bomb into Paris. You're a swindler, a liar and a disappointment—but not a murderer."

"Wow. That's what Rene said and he hardly knows me."

"*I* hardly know you."

"You knew everything worth knowing about me on our second date."

Another awkward silence follows while the wind bites and the snow flies hard in our faces. We start walking in the other direction, away from the wind, just to warm up.

"I'll get you a lawyer," she says, "a good one, instead of that connected idiot you've got. You can fight them."

"I can't fight this in court. It's impossible."

"You don't know that. There's something out there—"

"A *jury* is out there. The instant they release my name or picture, it's over for me. No matter what, I'm 'the Paris bomber'. 'We didn't realize how alienated he was—he seemed so quiet.' I already own *Catcher in the Rye*—they won't even have to plant it on my bookshelf."

"Those are just stories. The facts—"

"Stories are all we have anymore. Facts require research, detachment. The fear comes too fast now for that kind of process."

"But the facts are on your side!" And she thinks *I'm* stubborn! "You've got to see—"

"I don't *care* about facts!" I burst and she looks stunned. Really? *Really*? "*You're* the fact person here, not me! The network execs said you were 'difficult' and you held your head up and ignored them because the facts were on your side—and now you're freelance, scrounging for airtime from the assholes who didn't care about the facts."

"That's cruel," she says. I promised myself at the beginning I'd never make her cry—but then, I broke that vow a while ago.

"It's the *truth*," I say. "Facts just aren't enough anymore. It can't just be true—it's got to *sell*. The only way to fight a story is with a better story.

"I'm not taking any pleas," I hear myself say. "I'm *not* giving myself up. I've got to find whatever's behind this and prove my innocence."

It's a delirious and slightly ridiculous moment but I'm not addressing her anymore. I'm fully aware that I'm mouthing movie dialogue but I'm really just talking to myself—and to any force in the universe that might want to prevent a normally corrupt person like myself from being convicted of even worse shit than I've actually done. I know of no proof that any such force actually exists, but, for the moment, I'm groveling to it like a penitent in the Ganges.

Sara's boiling, so much so that she doesn't see the cone of snow collecting on the tip of her nose. I wipe it off—she nearly slugs me until she realizes what I'm doing. "You've got to get inside," I say and her eyes clear.

"So where do you need to go?" she says. "Figure it out, I'll wait. I'll get you there, *then* I'll go."

"Don't be a martyr!" Oops! Bad choice of words.

"Right, *you* be the martyr! Did you bring the bomb to Paris?"

"Of course not!"

"Does *anyone* believe you?"

"No!"

"Well, there we are. You're a hopeless case—my kind of story. What do we do about it?"

This is that same determination that got Sara fired from networks, plural, over the years. The famous story was that she promised the Israeli prime minister she wouldn't ask the question all the reporters wanted to ask. And got the interview specifically because of her promise. And then promptly asked the question anyway, the instant the cameras were rolling.

Which, come to think of it, means she *lied* to him. I take a ludicrous satisfaction in her hypocrisy.

`-That's what you were thinking about at`
`that moment? Proving her wrong?`

No, actually I was thinking about getting her back.

`-Then and there? In the moment?`

You bet. All of a sudden, I could really see it in front of me, a straight line ahead.

-You were willing to put her at risk to make that happen?

Either you haven't been listening or you'd know nobody ever puts Sara at risk for *anything*. Sara does what Sara wants.

And, to tell the truth, I *never* fully accept I'm going to fail at anything. I've been in big trouble before, not like this maybe but bad, and in the middle of my life going up in flames, I'm thinking about what to do when it all blows over, how to explain things, how I can take advantage. The odds are ridiculous but I'm trying to work the angles.

-Denial is a powerful form of ambition.

Exactly.

-And a river in Egypt.

I'll bet when they print the transcript, they leave out your jokes.

Anyway, so now I'm settling on a clear plan: there's somebody out there behind all this, pulling the strings. And I have to find him.

"Okay," I say. "I need your help."

"What?" It doesn't feel like a big deal to me but her eyes light up.

"I need you to call Diamante. We're divorced—I'll gamble that GIGN isn't tracking *your* phone. Ask him if he's seen Harry and if he's checked the boudoir. Tell him *exactly* that, make sure he's heard it, then hang up immediately."

"He'll understand that?"

"Yeah."

She's off the phone in seconds. "He was with people," she reports, hanging up. "I heard voices. He rushed me off."

"All the better."

"It sounds like the *flics* are there."

"That's okay—he got the message or he wouldn't have rushed you off."

"So now what?"

"Now I meet him and you go home."

Of course, I know better. She shakes her head immediately.

"No."

"Look—"

"*You* look. You're a total screw-up but I know you didn't do this," she says, taking control, as usual. "I've spent the last twenty years walking into dangerous situations for people who needed help. You need me."

"I can handle myself."

"I definitely improve your odds. Where's the boudoir?"

~~~

The boudoir is on the Rue Auger, a tiny cupola set back on a rooftop in the middle of the block. Harry's not here, either.

"What is this place?"

"Harry's second apartment, for trysts."

"He loves Diamante. He still has trysts?"

"Maybe. Maybe he just wants to think he still could."

I haven't been here a lot lately but the place doesn't look disturbed. A coffee cup sits in the sink and unspoiled milk in the door of the refrigerator.

"What are we searching for?"

"First off, his laptop."

"Where is it?"

"Usually on the table, right here." I've always loved the work nook under the round porthole window across from the fireplace. But no laptop.

I start pulling open bedroom drawers and check under the bed, just in case. Sara opens the kitchen cupboards—I've seen Harry stuff magazines, articles of clothing and even pairs of boots onto a kitchen shelf due to unexpected company. But no boots, no laptop.

And then the stairs creak and the door pops opens and Diamante hustles in, leather coat flapping.

"Did they follow you?"

"Of course, they followed me! I lost them in the bathroom at Gare du Nord, it's too dangerous for them. How the hell did we move a bomb?"

"I swear to God we didn't! I *hope* to God we didn't! Tell me you brought your laptop?"

He pulls it out of his bag. "Harry's not here? Now I'm worried."

"You didn't see him? Last night?"

He shakes his head. "I assumed he was here."

"Who can tell?" Harry couldn't make a bed if they were giving out prizes. "*Did* we move the bomb? Find out, find out!"

"Well, I guess we already know." Diamante pulls a sheet of paper from his jacket pocket. "The *flics* gave me this—it's a copy of the shipping certificate, signed by you, 'demolition equipment' to Baksheer Nimtokwu." He sees I'm drawing a blank. "You don't watch the news? The bomber. They shot him dead in a gunfight two hours ago in Nanterre."

I look over the cert. "Is it real? Someone forged my signature."

"I've done it," Diamante mutters, not looking up. Sara raises her hand as well.

Diamante's laptop boots. He sets up the VPN connection and waits for it to connect to our office system.

"How could we not know about this?"

"More to the point," Sara says, "how did the *flics* find it if you didn't know about it?" The question sits in the air for just a moment, until she answers. "Makes you think someone led them there, doesn't it?" As soon as she says it, it seems obvious.

"How?"

"That's the easy part," Diamante says, clicking away. "They hacked our system and added a cert."

"No, that wouldn't do it," I say. "It's got my signature."

"Forged."

"Even moreso. They didn't just stick on a phony signature, they got far enough into our system to find a genuine one to copy."

"So they edited one we'd already used. The question is, who benefits from you in jail?" Diamante asks.

"Or," Sara counters, "on the run. The guys that kidnapped us just wanted to keep us out of circulation."

"Kidnapped?"

"Proto Toulouanda and Rene Baudelaire took us for a ride. Literally. They dumped us as soon as they found out we were persons of interest. Those guys are pros—they don't take a piss without getting paid first. Whoever hired them didn't tell them anything about the bomb."

"Or didn't know about it," Sara says. "I think there's two strands—one wants you in jail, the other is afraid of what you might tell the police."

"I *know* something?" My thoughts jump immediately to Hastings and Mr. Woczynski but they want me loose, acquiring Dieter's little toys. "It's news to me, honest to God."

She sighs. "Or the kidnapping was a diversion, because there's evidence somewhere, here or in the office or Harry's apartment, that would prove your innocence?"

"Here's the cert," Diamante says, waiting for the document on the laptop screen to sharpen. He frowns at the result.

"What's the matter? Is it there?"

"It's here—but it's wrong."

We all gather in the light of the flickering screen.

"*What's* wrong?"

"Look—every cert carries a unique identifier, three three-digit sequences. The first set is right—"

"So, like you said, they hacked us."

"Yeah, but the middle three, we won't get to that sequence for another month or two."

"What's your point?" Diamante's understanding of machines and systems is far beyond that of us organic units. Everyone knows this but him.

"Why jump to a cert we weren't using? Why go to the trouble of figuring out and using next month's number sequence? How could you even *guess* that online?"

I grab Sara's phone out of her hand and hand it to Diamante. "Call the office."

Clarice answers and I take the phone from him.

"I need you to find a cert, right away. 942 762 837. It's not the regular book but it's got to be there someplace. Find it, take a picture of it and text it to this number right away!"

"What's going on?" Sara says when I ring off.

-Yes, what *is* going on? You've lost me.

Okay, sorry—the shipping business has been around a long time and shipping certs have not yet caught up with the digital age. We keep digital certificates in our records so we can do searches and check records off-site but in the vast majority of the world, you can't legally ship anything without a physical certificate—an actual piece of paper, a notarized form. Several copies, to be exact, at very least one for our paper files at the office and one that must be stored in the ship's manifest.

Diamante's point is, if someone just wanted to hack our system to produce a phony shipping cert, they would have edited one of our existing certificates and sent that to the cops. No reason there to find a real cert number we hadn't used yet.

–But if the theft was of a real paper certificate–

See? You *are* a detective. If it's paper, they would need one we hadn't used—and, if they didn't want us to notice, one from next month would be ideal.

–So did that suggest your innocence?

Actually, the opposite. It suggests that someone used one of our real, legal-document certs to really ship the bomb to Paris.

–Oh.

Yeah—oh. *That* takes the wind out of all our sails. Now we're waiting for Clarice to ring back with what might be horrible news. That kind of waiting is terrible. Time just gasps and collapses in the corner.

Finally, I feel a buzz in my palm. There's a picture, though it takes a second to resolve on screen.

"It's a real cert," I groan.

Except it isn't.

"It's the same number—and signature—as the one Diamante got from the police. But it's not going to Paris."

The cert shows a small container assigned to a ship, the *Mercury Venture.*

*"Mercury Venture—*I know that name," Diamante says, and clicks through our database. "Small freighter, we've used it before. Notes say it left Karachi this morning for Hong Kong. Scheduled to arrive in three weeks."

"But it's the same number as the Paris cert."

"They couldn't use it for both?" Sara asks.

Diamante shakes his head. "There's only one paper cert. They made it look like they were shipping to Hong Kong so we wouldn't stop the bomb to Paris."

My heart sinks. This is terrible. I can't see a way out of this.

"But—it's dated just a couple of days ago," Sara says. "Does that make any sense?

"Huh?"

"They said the *Rue Breguet* bomb was huge. Wouldn't somebody have noticed something that big being delivered all at once? Wouldn't they have brought it in in bits and pieces over time?"

"Maybe this was the biggest piece," I say listlessly. "What's the difference?"

"No," Diamante's eyes are bright. "Doesn't it make more sense—" He's shaking his head—and pounding his keyboard again.

"—if it's the *opposite*?" Sara says.

"What if the real paper cert is for the shipment on the *Mercury Venture*," Diamante adds, "carrying construction equipment to Hong Kong?" He burrows through our records. "If it's a real container of ours," he says, "it'll have a tracker."

As soon as he says 'tracker', the word begins ringing over and over in my head—and I finally remember why. "Diamante, didn't you put a tracker on *Harry*?"

"What?"

"Last week, when you said he was getting wobbly, you said you put a tracker on Harry's phone, in case he forgot who he was and wandered off. Did you—?"

"Did I actually do it or just think about it?" He stops typing in mid-sentence and hands me his phone. "If I installed it, it'll be on my desktop." He goes back to searching. "The tracker will show us how far the ship is from Hong Kong. We can get them to stop at the nearest port to verify the shipment."

"None of this matters, really," I whine. "Nobody's going to buy this story even if the container's real."

"Maybe *Harry*," Sara says, "would know something about it—if we knew where he was." She's staring at me, expectant. And there is a tracker app on Diamante's desktop, so I activate it.

"I still say he could be kidnapped," she repeats.

"Like I said, no ransom demands, no kidnapping."

Diamante throws up his hands in frustration.

"What?"

"Stupid app. It confirms the container as listed on the cert and it confirms the ship."

"Isn't that good news?" I can't tell anymore.

"Sure. The bad news is, it shows the *Mercury Venture* sailing south into the Persian Gulf out of Basra."

"Basra—*Iraq*?"

"Yup."

"Pardon me, but if you're on your way from Karachi to Hong Kong, isn't that the total fucking wrong direction?"

"Tell me about it."

"Is it a smokescreen?" Sara asks.

"For what? It's a ship carrying one of our containers. Why isn't it where it's supposed to be?"

A long deadly pause now, as we all absorb this.

"And where is Harry?" Sara asks, unable to stop beating the dead horse.

The map is onscreen but I have to look twice, then zoom out for a better view, to understand what I'm seeing. "Oh!"

"Where the fuck is he?"

"According to this, he's in Saudi Arabia."

ALLIES

"What's he doing in Saudi Arabia?"

"Well, actually, no." I zoom in on the map. "He's in Qumradhi, actually. Just south of Saudi Arabia."

"And your ship," Sara says, "is in the Persian Gulf?"

"Steaming South out of Iraq," Diamante says.

"Heading straight for Qumradhi."

"Somebody's kidnapped Harry," Sara continues, the horse having risen miraculously from the dead, "and is delivering something to him in Qumradhi."

"You don't kidnap somebody to deliver something to him," I say. "They set up the shipment and kidnapped him to make sure nothing goes wrong."

"Shipment of what? What's 'Construction equipment'?"

"It's just a catch-all category we use."

"Covering what?"

"Oh, a wide variety—"

"How wide?"

There's no way to sugar-coat it. "The mind boggles."

Sara rolls her eyes. "Well, Harry's phone didn't go to Qumradhi without him. We have to go there, too."

And now my stomach sinks. I don't like this one bit.

I expected, when we got to this moment, that I'd find an angry partner at the other end of the chain, some arrogant weasel demanding revenge or compensation for whatever wrong we'd done him. Someone we'd probably already played, whose strengths and weaknesses would be familiar, maybe even predictable. I'd expected, at very least, to be able to estimate by now the cost of making the problem go away.

Which is to say, I'd expected this to be just another episode in our closed little game. All this time, I've qualified and vetted every person who entered our circle, limited our professional contacts to a narrow sequence of tightly controlled interactions, all guided by HARRY'S RULES. Anyone in our game danced our dance and whenever things began to diverge from plan, I had a contingency to pull us out, but quick.

The benefit of a tightly controlled game is, you limit risk. We've managed to stay *safe*, in a uniquely unsafe profession.

Clearly, that safety is all gone now. Dragging Harry off to the Middle East? Hacking our records? Forging certs? I feel totally out of my league. Whoever thought this one up has imagination a whole order of magnitude larger than anything I've ever possessed.

There's no signpost here for me to lean on. I feel like someone just woke me up standing on a 98th floor balcony rail and yelled, "Dance!"

Diamante and Sara are staring at me, awaiting direction. That's my job, it's who I've always been. All I can think to say at the moment is, "Yeah, I guess we have to go."

"The trip requires a passport," Diamante reminds me. "You don't have yours on you, do you?"

"I don't have a *wallet* at the moment."

"Going home to pick it up would be a bad idea," Sara says, leading to a long silence.

I stare out the round window, across the tile roof and the smoke rising from the chimneys. My mind's churning in low gear but my history is to solve problems—it's the way I think. If I can't solve big ones, I'll go one step at a time, because what else is there?

"Call Nassir, Sonya's son," I tell Diamante. "Get him to run her by the office."

"If GGIN is staking it out—"

"We'll have to take the chance. She's just dropping by, she left her sweater behind. If there's cops, pick up the sweater and get the hell out. If they haven't locked it off, have her pick up the folder we got from the Hastings meeting. Take several other folders—in case they catch her on the way out, she can say—"

"I've got the folder," Diamante says. He sees my surprise. "I wasn't leaving it around the office while the *flics* searched. I dumped the bag with it down the laundry chute." He hands me the manila envelope.

"Okay, we need a car—"

"I've got a car." Who knew the man had a car? You think you know a person and then you find out they can drive!

"You don't happen to have any large plastic shipping containers on you?" I ask.

"No—you've got me there," he smiles.

"Fine," I say, ignoring the questions on both their faces. "We can pick them up on the way to the airport."

~~~

"I'm just saying, you can't use the airport. This is the first place they'll be watching," Sara repeats.

"My job is to know where opportunity lies," I say. She doesn't seem impressed.

Diamante's car is an ancient *Deux Chevaux*. We couldn't outrun a Vespa, but no one's likely to consider this clapped-out relic a getaway car.

"You're not listening to me," she complains.

"I'm listening—I just don't have time to explain my brilliant plan."

"Your brilliant plan, which consists of three suitcases filled with socks."

"Socks in boxes, that are solid and won't shift around very much. They're props. The plan is—" I check the Parker Meridien passports and ID's that I'm completing with our new drug store photos. "The plan is, you are Chris Dale, Parker Meridien sales manager and you're accompanying us on a preview of the new spring initiative."

"What's Parker Meridien selling this spring?"

"Let's say, a new infrared targeting system for your drones, improved bluetooth communications for your security guards and a radiation detector app for your smartphone. Okay?"

"And what if I'm recognized?"

I pull a plastic case out of the shopping bag.

"What's this?"

"A jean jacket with sequins and lots of cheap makeup. Slather it on. Make yourself Clown Barbie."

"Ooh! Do we have ten minutes? Can I tease my hair into a bouffant?"

"You can do that in ten minutes?"

"There's the terminal," she points helpfully as we drive past.

"That's not where we're going," I say, enjoying her confusion.

Diamante assured me the makeup alone would do the job and I've got to admit, I wouldn't recognize Sara when she steps out of the car. This is a woman with very little money and even less taste and at least one of those would have made me reconsider marrying her.

We drive past all the usual entrances to the airport and finally come around the back way, where Diamante's Sandler & Son shipper's ID card gets us through the unmanned gate. Then we take the internal roads to the rear entrance of our terminal.

We enter through the shipping area, a freeway cloverleaf of conveyor belts and motorized carriages rapidly filling and rushing out to flights waiting to be released.

"*Bonsoir*, Abdul."

"Nicky! What do you have for me?"

Abdul runs the baggage service for this terminal. From experience, I know that this day and hour is traditionally one of his worst and everything we see confirms that. The place is jam-packed and frenzied, staff trying desperately to yell over the never-ending din of equipment. As we barrel up to his counter, wheeling our big suitcases, it's beyond chaos and Abdul is totally out of his depth—my favorite kind of baggage manager and worth every penny we've spent over the years bribing him.

"Three to be personally delivered on Flight 323. We have to see them on and see them off."

"323? The gate's probably closed already. Where are your couriers?"

-What is this about, please? What does 'Personally delivered' mean?

There's a huge high-end business sending couriers around the world personally accompanying items that are too precious to be shipped. The personal touch and personal—bonded—responsibility. When expensive items are too big to be carried in hand luggage, the couriers can be given permission to witness the luggage compartment of the plane being locked on the outbound leg with their bags inside and unlocked when they arrive at the other end, with the chain of personal custody undisturbed. So now, we're asking Abdul to get us—and our personally-supervised parcels—onto a flight that's almost finished boarding, at the very last minute.

"We're the couriers. Can't get anybody on short notice."

"This is crazy timing, Nicky."

"Yeah, I know. Listen, Abdul, couldn't you—"

"Nicky, you know I can't—if somebody asks questions—"

"Who's going to ask about us? C'mon, just this once. I haven't asked for a favor in weeks!" *And I've been paying you for them for years*, I think but don't say.

-What favor?

We have tickets for the flight (in our cover names) but clearly, we haven't gone through boarding and security like we should have. I'm asking Abdul to skip that step and send us to watch the cargo load and then directly up the jetramp, which he's not supposed to do, of course. However, I know he's done it before, with couriers he knows and I've shipped probably two thousand packages with him over the years, so I'm hoping—really hoping—he'll help me slip through the system this one time.

But he's uncertain. This is a man who never stops moving and now he's slumped, immobile, in place as the parcels fly into bins all around him.

"Abdul—I'll give you the Aeroflot."

He remains slumped over the counter but somehow his body rises, as though levitating in place. "Don't toy with me, Nicky," he says.

"It's a big client and neither of us has time. Just help me out. I'll give you the whole set."

Airlines used to use actual china cups and plates and real silver cutlery on long-distance flights—this is back when dinosaurs roamed the Earth, of course. So naturally, now the old service sets are cult items on Ebay and Etsy, especially if you can find them in the original boxes. And especially if we're talking Soviet-era Aeroflot, where the boxes have nice pictures of Lenin and Brezhnev and an entire flight full of passengers was once forced to search the floor of the cabin on their hands and knees because a real silver fork-and-knife set was lost and the crew were not willing to find themselves permanently relocated to Irkutsk.

"It's at the office," I assure him. "I'll get it for you as soon as I get back."

"You swear this to me. On your honor as a man."

"I'll throw in a Gorbachev flight pin. But get us on this plane."

"I'll do it!" Abdul almost snaps to attention. "Kwame! Three for the 323 to Heathrow. Nicky, take that tractor directly to the ramp, I'll let them know you're coming."

"Thanks. And they'll let us off to see them unlock on the other side—you'll tell the crew, okay?"

"You'll throw in the salt and pepper shakers?"

"They're no good to me if I'm giving away the rest of the set."

"Fly well, my friend."

A moment later, we're on a luggage tram, hurtling across the tarmac to the underside of Flight 323, the next plane to Heathrow. We watch our bags swallowed by the luggage compartment and locked for flight. Then we walk around to the jetramp, up the steps to the front hatch of the plane, the crew check our seat assignments—but nothing else—and we're off.

"And at the other end?" Sara asks once we're seated.

"They'll take us off the flight ahead of everyone else, down the steps to the runway, we'll see the luggage compartment unloaded. And, since I know Martin Fosgate at Heathrow, we'll take one of the luggage trolleys to the freight receiving area and walk directly out of there to the taxi row. No security at either end."

"So why don't we just fly to Qumrahdi—why Heathrow?"

"Because that's an international flight—Customs. Abdul won't fuck with Customs, even for Aeroflot salt shakers."

"So how will we get around them?" she asks.

"In England, we'll wrangle ourselves an invisible plane."

DIVERSION

France's snow was delightful next to England's fog and wind-driven hail. The mist cuts off the hills mid-chest, sky and earth a watercolor merge through windshield splatter.

"Where is this place?" Sara asks.

"You'll know it when you see it."

On the seat between us is a London tabloid. The headline reads:

MYSTERY MAN!

"They don't have your name yet," Diamante reads. "Just 'French authorities are seeking a Paris resident of ten years, accused of material support to the Rue Breguet bombing.' We have to get to Harry immediately."

"'Immediately' is whatever's most inconspicuous," I say.

"You call a flat-bed truck inconspicuous?" Sara hasn't been comfortable since the rental counter.

"It'll be worse once we fill it. We don't have a choice. The invisible plane requires cargo."

We crest the hill and come to a stop in front of the two-story shiny-black wrought-iron gate separating the Linden estate from the mouth-breathers.

I punch the intercom button on the gate. "It's Nicky Marsh for the Duke, please. Tell him it's an emergency."

A couple of minutes pass, followed by, "Compliments from the Duke, Mr. Marsh, but he wishes me to ask, what precisely is the emergency?"

"The emergency is, I have his money!"

The gate opens.

The long driveway reveals the estate in stages, a green copper dome rising above a circular valley and a peek-a-boo eighteenth-century manor house placed carefully between rows of ancient oaks.

Daniel Fortescu Gael Winthrop Davis-Giddle, the 14th Duke of Linden, steps onto the pebbled drive as we approach, under a voluminous umbrella held by a manservant his grandfather's age. It was actually safe to assume he'd be home—being a Duke these days means hustling tour groups, weddings and movie shoots through the estate almost daily, to keep the roof from leaking and the walls from collapsing. At least, that's how he tells it. He shakes my hand unconvincingly, like an inbred English lord should.

"Which money is this, Nicky?"

"Your ship has come in, Larry (with all his names, everyone calls him Larry—real aristocracy is the only possible explanation for this). I've come for the 917."

"I've told you before, I can't give it away. It's wearing a hole in my pocket but..."

"Buy yourself two pair of slacks. This buyer will meet your price." Larry and I have buzzed around this subject five times in as many years, with three different suitors.

"You're aware of my *new* price, are you?" Good Lord, without dropping a beat! What a fucker! We reached an impasse a month ago over a couple of thousand. He had his price and my client was an ass—I respected Larry for that. But not this!

"How much more?" I ask and he tells me—almost 10%. "Why?"

"Inflation."

"There's no inflation."

"There's bound to be eventually."

Tick tick tick. It takes me just that long to realize I'm an idiot—I'm worrying about the price! We need to get to Harry and the 917 is the only way I can think to rig it. And, not insignificantly, it's not my money anyway.

Even if it was, the car would still be a bargain. Larry has no idea what he has. His 917 was painted over before he bought it, in the blue and yellow Gulf Oil livery used by Steve McQueen in his quixotic 'Le Mans' movie (you want a movie that *works*? Start with an actual script! Next question...) instead of the flaming red-and-white it originally carried—the red-and-white worn presently by a replica in the Porsche museum. Larry thinks he has a movie car, missing the fact that he actually owns the real-life race winner, the first Porsche to win Le Mans.

"I'll accept your price," I tell him. "Bank transfer okay?" It's worth an extra 10% just to see Larry's face drop—he knows instantly he should have asked for more. "C'mon Larry, it's six less tour groups this year."

"You've no idea what it takes to keep a place like this!" he moans. "I have a whole wing that needs repointing! The boathouse is sinking!"

"Is there a boat in it?"

"What's the point of a boathouse?"

"Then don't ask me for sympathy." I hand him Diamante's phone. "Punch in your bank account here. You should be ashamed, hustling me."

"I'm not," he answers, punching in the number and holding it out to me expectantly. I shake my head—*not so fast, buddy.*

"Where's the car?"

"You want it *now*?"

I panic for a moment. "It's here, isn't it?"

"Of course, it's here!" he declares with all the wounded honor of the ancestors who actually died for the place—or who at least waved their peons in the direction of the battle so *they* could die for the place. "I just have to dig it out."

Dig it out?

It takes several minutes just to open the garage alongside the stables. I suspect Larry's taking his time, trying to find an excuse to charge me more but eventually, the locks give and he slides the door open, revealing a Ferrari 250 GTO, two Mercedes 300 SL's (a convertible and gullwing coupe), a Lotus 72 in John Player black and gold (Fittipaldi), a gray Duesenberg convertible, a 1965 Alfa Giulia with no rust (none! In England, no less!) and a silver 1947 Delahaye coupe, maybe the most outrageous car I've ever seen. Larry supervises his staff (who materialize out of nowhere) carefully shuffling the cars to get to the 917.

"I think you're overplaying your poverty, Larry."

"They're investments. I'm cash-poor."

"That's a white man's problem," Diamante mutters as we finally reach the car.

Pardon me—the CAR!!!!

It's a 917K, alright—a shark's face, brutal-looking, thigh-high, crude and shrieking once we hook up the portable starter and make sure all twelve cylinders still light. Oh, do they ever.

With that, Diamante holds his finger over the 'transfer' button.

I hold my breath and take Larry's place in the driver's seat—if Hastings or Woczynski set the cops on me, they'll surely have canceled my access to the accounts. In which case—? In which case, I tell Larry the transfer went through and hope he can't stop me before I've sped past his gates.

I tried calling Woczynski on the way here. His assistant said, "You don't need to speak to him" and hung up. Which isn't the same as "He's not speaking to you." At least, I hope it's not the same.

At the last second, I take the phone from Diamante and attach a note to the payment saying it's for 'Porsche 917K'—if Woczynski reads notes, which I doubt, maybe that'll make a difference.

Then I push the button. And, after just a short delay, hear a beep from Larry's phone. He clicks his home screen and smiles.

We sign documents so it's really legal and Diamante and I hustle the thing onto the trailer.

Once we're on the road again, I call ahead. "Staff Sergeant Hector Lopez, please. Hector, I'm with Parker Meridien. Dieter Miller said we should call you—we're transporting a car, to Qumradhi, Wadiirah—today, if at all possible."

—So this Staff Sergeant Lopez, he was in on the scheme?

Staff Sergeant Lopez is the loadmaster on a C5A military transport plane, moving whatever the spooks and contractors tell him to and not asking questions. He is also, happily for us, a supreme geekboy. He asks what our cargo weighs and if it needs any special handling. When I tell him it's a 1970 Porsche 917K, he's a six-year-old boy with a Lego set. Do I know the nose clearance off the top of my head? Because he won't take a chance on scraping the precious nose, getting the Porsche onto his plane. He's wants to build hydraulic mounts under the wheels so the thing won't get jostled in flight—he makes it sound like he does this every day and maybe he does. If he could tailor a custom mink-lined car cover for us in the time available, it's clear he would. "I'll meet you at the gate," he says, "so you won't get dicked around at the guardhouse."

**-You feel more confident on a military
flight than civilian?**

Well, military, civilian, that's really neither here nor
there. The money transfer went through with Larry, which
gives   me   some   confidence   that   the
Hastings/Dieter/Woczynski axis isn't hunting me, at least
not for the moment. And if they're on my side, this is my
best chance of getting to where Harry is.

**-Even if they know you're trying to
escape the Paris police?**

Well, the odds are at least 50/50 they *don't* know, since
I haven't made the papers yet. But truthfully? I don't think
they'd care one bit, as long as I'm delivering Dieter's 917.

True to his word, Hector is at the gate when we reach
RAF Mildenhall. The base is a through-the-looking-glass
slice of America dumped into the Suffolk countryside. Right
up to the gate, you're still in normal English suburbs—
hedgerows lining narrow roads, hatchbacks and little mini-
trucks driving on the left, mom and pop stores and narrow
houses with slate roofs. As soon as you pass inside the gate,
it's pimped-out Mustangs and huge Ford F-150's driving on
the *right*, Burger King, Taco Bell, Domino's, an American

supermarket, even American-style fire hydrants on the corners.

Hector rides the running board of our flatbed, giving directions as we cross through the base town. He's totally starstruck over the 917 and I think, *I want this guy on our side*. As we near the runway complex, I pull over and point to the race car.

"You wanna ride out to the plane?"

"Not a chance—they'd bust me out for that!" he says. "*Nobody* drives onto the flight line." Then he gets that lovely larcenous look in his eye, the one that's kept me in the black all these years. "You could take me the back way—around the service road."

"You won't get busted for that??"

"You drive me up to the gate, no problem. Everybody uses the service road for drag racing on the weekends."

Diamante and I unhook and carefully roll the 917 off the truck. With an expanse of curving service road laid out in front of me, we take our seats, I fire her up, take firm hold of the steering wheel and push on the pedal.

It's amazing, if you like being shot out of a cannon. Hector slams back into the firewall with a huge smile on his face. The Porsche has no speedometer so I don't know how fast we're going but I dump the accelerator after four or five seconds—that's all we need—and we coast the rest of the way to the checkpoint. Then Diamante and I load her back onto the flatbed for the short trip to the C5. It's not like anyone has to point it out—a C5 is the height of a six-story building, with a wingspan the size of Big Ben.

The plane stands open clamshell-style, nose cone high in the air, a metal ramp drooping to the ground like a tongue. An absurd collection of hardware waits at attention to be loaded on this behemoth—a tank the size of a seaside bungalow, six portable generators on wheels, a palette in plastic wrap with white powder puffing from the seams, a gorgeous antique mahogany power cruiser and a military helicopter (!), its rotors all folded in the same direction and locked down for travel.

"That was fantastic!" Hector yelps, uncoiling himself from the car. "Does this thing have any sort of self-leveling?"

"It was built in 1968. We're lucky it has brakes."

"Okay, we'll build a ramp."

He fiddles with two-by-fours and little planks of wood for twenty minutes, just so our precious baby makes it up onto the ramp without a scrape. I feel brilliant until he spends three hours putting the same laborious effort into loading all the other items into the cargo bay.

The plane is scheduled for Dubai and I wouldn't argue—my main concern for now is to get the hell out of Europe—but, after the pilots ogle the Porsche and attempt to sit inside (over 5'10", don't bother), everyone decides Qumradhi is less than an hour out of the way and add it to the flight plan.

After that, it's just waiting. Waiting for the gatehouse guards to realize they've been hoodwinked or the pilots to get a security bulletin or for some well-connected spook onboard to get inside information and call us out. I've managed to hold myself in check all the way here, focusing on one task after another. But now, every few minutes, some noise—a car starting, a siren, a plane taxiing across the field—makes me jump. I use the stinking Air Force toilet three times on the runway (ignoring signs to the contrary) before engine start.

Finally, the load-up is complete and maybe twenty of us climb a short ladder and a long staircase to the upper level of the plane, where ridiculously comfortable seats for 75 await. The engines turn, we rumble down the runway and finally take flight. Six hours to Qumrahdi. Six hours to figure out what to do next.

DREAMS

"You take the apartment." I tell Sara.

"What?"

Somehow, I slept. It's a small miracle. On a military plane in flight, totally wound up, somehow I'd slept for several hours and dreamed of our endless apartment above the garden of the *Hopital Saint-Louis*—many more rooms than actually exist. Of course, it was a dream. All I know is, far too many empty rooms for me.

"What are you talking about?" She seems drowsy too. How many hours were we up together before the plane? Was I sleeping on her shoulder? "The lawyers settled all that. You get the apartment, I get the furnishings. You said you didn't want to dicker over the details."

"Yeah, well, I'll trade you the apartment for the TV, the Weegee photo and the mattress. You know you aren't going to keep the mattress, it's a reminder of me."

She considers a snarky reply, I can see it on her face—I know that expression, I love that expression, like all her expressions—but she abandons it. Have I become that pathetic? *C'mon, wrestle with me a little.*

"Why the change of heart?" she asks. "You loved that apartment."

"I thought I did. I guess I just didn't want to spend months arguing over things." She still seems troubled. "If you love it—"

"It's too much for one person," she says, a touch resentfully. "It's right for two."

And that's the answer. Of course it is. Another awkward pause, the ones we've become so used to in the last few months.

"Nobody's come around—asking questions? Looking us over?" I say.

"I was sleeping too. We're in flight—aren't we okay for now?"

"They could have gotten a bulletin in flight. Somebody could have read something before coming on board and recognized us."

She considers this for a moment. "Okay—and what can we do about it? Do you know where they keep the parachutes?"

"I bet they've got bins full of them," I mutter but that doesn't get us any closer to finding any.

Why is she staring at me?

"What's *wrong* with you?" she asks finally and I'm trying to figure out if it's a general question or something specific. "I'm trying, I really am. I'm usually good at understanding people, but you? You can be so generous—you buy me a horse I desperately want and would never imagine buying, you offer me back an apartment you could easily sell. But you cheat people for a living. You're a paranoid and a swindler. How did that happen?"

"I'm *not* a swindler." She snorts a laugh but I don't blink. "Harry, whom you love—"

"I do."

"*Harry* is a swindler. I'm the guy who totes the odds. I'm the guy who checks out the prospects, figures out what they want and what they can afford to lose without it hurting too much."

"So—you're his enabler?"

"I'm the guy who makes it safe."

"For the world?"

"Fuck the world—the world can take care of itself. I make it safe for Harry."

She stares for a while and, when she speaks, it's a quiet voice, not accusing, just trying to understand. "Why? Why screw the rest of the world for Harry?"

"I'm not screwing the rest of the world, I'm just not watching out for them. I watch out for Harry because he saved my life."

MEETING

I met Harry in Nassau, in the Bahamas. I was rootless, two years after my disgrace in front of a congressional committee. I was finally walking down the street without wondering whether passersby were more likely to be thinking 'traitor' or 'imbecile.' I'd done a few writing jobs and a little bartending but I had no purpose in life and I'd stopped looking for any.

And then I saw Alec Broadmoor step out of a taxi with a trophy blond and six suitcases, heading into the most expensive hotel on the island. Broadmoor was the Chief of Staff for the Intelligence Committee, the little shit who instigated our assistance to the freedom fighters and led the grilling when it proved bad politics. Five-foot-four in his stocking feet and, at that size, towering over his moral footprint.

I stopped dead staring at him, my heart pounding, two years of fantasized rage rushing out of me.

The fucker had to pay.

I had to kill him, kill him cruelly, slowly, rip his heart out of his chest with my bare hands and make him eat it. Okay, maybe that was a bit much. At very least, I should be able to shoot him with a sniper rifle from half a mile away and be gone by the time someone had to clean up the mess.

Suddenly, I had a plan and a purpose. I shadowed him for a day and a half, not sleeping, barely eating, until I knew his schedule, who he saw, where and what he ate and how frequently he went to the bathroom (much too often for the call of nature, which didn't shock me).

I fixed on three locations where I could shoot him at a convenient distance and be out of the neighborhood before anyone noticed. I found a shop where I could purchase an accurate rifle with a good sight and no records and a furnace nearby that would melt the rifle beyond recognition in less than a minute. I had everything—except the constitution required of an assassin.

Sitting on a terrace overlooking his hotel, I had to face the fact that, unless it was self-defense, I just wasn't capable of killing anybody, even that puny piece of shit.

I can't remember feeling more disillusioned with myself. I felt totally defeated. I had the most venal piece of scum in the galaxy by the throat and I was going to let him go. I felt useless, impotent, screaming with frustration. It was the moment you realized you just couldn't bring yourself to take advantage of the drunken sorority girl—you know you're doing right, but what you hear most clearly in your head are the fraternity brothers calling you 'pussy'.

That was when Harry Grinnell (that was his name then) sat down at the table next to me, alongside a woman I remember only as Judy.

"Darling, if you love your son, why waste his best years over some archaic tradition?" said Harry, in a seersucker suit and silk neckerchief, cool as an iceberg despite the heat.

"We're British," said Judy, 40ish and not only well-dressed, but well-dressed as a woman of 40, meaning she had class and probably real money. "Archaic traditions are all we have left."

"The real issue is, she wasn't raised to be Sovereign and he was—I believe she resents that."

"Does *he* think so?"

"He wouldn't tell me if he did."

"Would she prefer William, when he comes of age? Would that devastate poor Charles?"

"You mustn't speak of him in those terms. He will be King. She will do the conventional thing through gritted teeth, as always."

"He might be happier *not* being King."

"He is the child of both parents," Harry sighed, looking through her as though Charles were there on the terrace, seeking their counsel. "He will do his duty."

By this point, I'd ordered lunch, even though I wasn't the slightest bit hungry. I'd never met anyone like Harry but I recognized the silhouette and knew, somehow, that this was a door opening for me.

He spun a great yarn. It was like hearing Ella Fitzgerald or Mel Torme scat—improvisation of a very high order and hopelessly easy to get caught up in. If you thought about it analytically, there were all sorts of holes, but Harry didn't allow that sort of analysis. Every phrase appeared as a combination of high gossip and affairs-of-state secrecy.

In less than fifteen minutes, he created a world where Charles was clearly a dear friend (though he never said so in so many words), the protector of a cherished past, set upon by all sides, an embattled idealist in need of champions.

And the means to support Charles, once it finally appeared, turned out to be a horse Harry was syndicating in Ireland—of which he broadly hinted Charles was part owner. The story was ludicrous. How any of it might actually help Charles was never clear.

Nor did any of that matter, really. Judy was a pile of goo on the floor by the time he finished his pitch, aching to serve in any capacity Harry could arrange. And if I'd had any money, I might have put some up, just in admiration for the way the story was put over.

I may not know Art, but I know what sells and this was it. So right then, I switched from shadowing Broadmoor to shadowing Harry. Just long enough to find out where he was staying and make sure he wasn't local mob. I made sure to keep my distance. I figured he'd be tougher to follow than

Broadmoor but he was surprisingly casual, even a bit careless.

The next morning, he was having breakfast on that same terrace when I sat down next to him.

"So?" he asked. "Do I have to buy you off or scare you off?" He gave me a moment to answer and then went on when I didn't. "I saw you following me yesterday so I knew we'd have a reckon at some point. You're not a friend of Judy's, you're not a cop. What's your game?"

I already felt out of my depth but I held myself together and made *my* pitch.

"I have a job for you," I told him. "It'll pay you lots more than Judy will."

He looked a bit cross-eyed for a moment. "What kind of job?"

"US Government bureaucrat, ambitious, a prick and blinded by his own ambition. I want you to take him."

"Why don't *you* take him?"

"Because you know *how*. Besides, he knows me. We were friends once." I watched him soak that up. "You take him and show me how. Because there's a few more besides him that owe me bigtime."

"I'm sorry, dear boy. I don't need a partner. I like to pick my own marks."

"I'll be an apprentice, just till I know how, then I'll go off on my own. I won't encroach on your territory."

At this, Harry motioned for the waiter and ordered a glass of expensive wine, leaving no doubt he expected me to pay.

"What do you think," he said with a sigh, "I'm going to give you a course? Bunko 101? You don't learn this sort of thing overnight and besides, you have to be the right sort of person, understand how things work."

"I am."

"Not blundering up to me like this. Besides, you don't have the instincts. You've told me nothing of value about this fellow."

"I've told you he's greedy and impulsive; both of those will override his judgment. He'll rush headlong if he's tempted and then rush to cover his tracks after the fact. He won't care about us, only about making sure no one else finds out."

His eyes narrowed. "Alright, that's useful—if it's true. What else do you know?"

"I know what he wants. What he *really* wants." I dropped a handful of coins on the table. "*That* is your play," I said, pointing at one of the coins.

It was the first time I saw him peering at me over his glasses, like a hawk eyeing a mouse. He picked up the coin and turned it over in his hand.

"I see— 'Confederate States of America', very nice. Why am I excited?"

"You're not but he will be. If that was real—"

"Which, clearly, it's not—"

"—If it was real, it would be the fifth of its kind in existence, a Confederate half-dollar piece. Two of the others sold at auction recently for around $600,000 apiece. This is a restrike made in the 1870's by a man who bought the only existing plates. It's worth around $3,000."

"Broadmoor knows about the real ones?"

"He does. I got this one from my ex-father-in-law, whose great-grandfather survived Pickett's Charge at Gettysburg. Broadmoor pestered me to see it for months at one point."

"Are we depending on him not knowing a real one from a fake?"

"Nope. There are only four real ones, very few photos even online, even the experts admit they'd need to examine the coins to tell the real ones from the restrikes. The only credibility issue is that the mint recorded only four coins being struck before they ran short of bullion."

Harry grimaced. "That is a problem. So why should he believe me when I tell him it's incredibly valuable?"

"Because you won't. He eats lunch at Mimo's clam bar every day—Mimo has a souvenir and jewelry shop with a big case of coins and trinkets from local shipwrecks. You'll go in while Broadmoor's having lunch and offer Mimo a bunch of coins you found on a dive a mile off Green Turtle Cay. You'll point out the one that says 'Confederate States' on it. That'll draw Broadmoor, I'll guarantee you."

"And he'll offer me big money just for that?"

"No, what I'm thinking is, you'll offer him all the coins for a couple hundred dollars." *Now* Harry was intrigued—his eyes lit up like candles. "You'll take his money and then say something like, 'If I'd known they were worth this much, I'd have taken all the other ones.'"

Harry's smiling broadly at this point. He leaned back in his chair, relaxed and enjoying. "Go on," he goaded.

"In 1861, the USS *San Jacinto* seized the Confederate Ambassadors to Britain and France off a ship in Havana and took them to prison in the North. In 1865, the *San Jacinto* sank off Green Turtle Cay, disintegrating in rough water so that most of her onboard stores were scattered all over the ocean floor there."

Again, Harry's eyes peering over the glasses, but this time with a conspiratorial twinkle. "And we're meant to convince Mr. Broadmoor that a secret cache of Confederate coinage was seized with the Ambassadors by, shall we say, a corrupt captain or First Mate—a cache that went down with the ship?"

"Actually, he already believes it. At least, he believes it's possible. He told me the story as he was planning a vacation down here, just before he decided to crucify me instead."

Harry withdrew, considering, for a moment. "And why wouldn't the mate have saved the coins when the ship sank?"

"Because, in 1865, once the war ended, they were worthless."

Harry returned to considering. It was lovely to watch his wheels turn. He clearly enjoyed the pleasures of a good plot.

"I will admit," he said finally, "you know how to bait the hook. I'm still holding the line, however. Why should I take the risk?"

"Because he's way richer than Judy and far less likely to do anything about it. He'll never admit that he's been taken, his pride is too strong. So it's a better haul and a safer one. And—if this goes well and you're interested—there are two more just like him that we can take later."

He stared at me for a long moment. "You'll give me a day to check out this fellow?"

"You could just take him yourself—once I give you his name, you don't really need me, do you?"

"I give you my word as a gentleman," he said solemnly, extending his hand. Then he burst out laughing. "I suppose that's a bit over the top, isn't it? How about my word as a scoundrel?"

We shook hands.

THE PROTECTED

And from then, my life changed.

Harry gave me my life back. He gave me agency, the sense that I could do something, that I could stand up for something, even if all I stood up for was swindlery (is that a word? If not, I want credit for it! Who do I know on the Oxford committee?).

"And then he taught you HARRY'S RULES," Sara says.

"Well, no," I admit through gritted teeth. "There are no HARRY'S RULES, really. I made up HARRY'S RULES once we started working together."

This is a very sensitive moment. The first time I tried explaining HARRY'S RULES to Sara, it broke up our marriage. I thought I was filling in the details to something she already understood. I was very wrong about that and now I worry that, with this admission, I'm picking at the scab.

"Like I said, Harry's the swindler. He's *never* had any rules—he's always made it up on the fly, taken his chances and went to jail when things went bad. It's all part of the game for him."

"But not for you?"

"Not for me. I did the same thing with Harry that I did with you—I took a leap of faith, impulsively, and then spent every moment after trying to make it safe, buff away the risks, rationalize all the things that excited me in the first place. I saw something I wanted but never expected to actually get—when I did, it scared the shit out of me."

"You don't trust the truth, why should you trust people?" she says and I feel myself redden.

"I just always feel like I have to improve the odds."

"How's that working out for you?" she asks and I have no answer. She holds up her phone. "I did a series on Qumrahdi when they unveiled the new downtown a few years ago. There's a tiny ruling family who own everything, flaunt their wealth, their own people hate them but get paid heavily just for being citizens. There's a huge population of foreign workers stranded there, sixty to a two-bedroom apartment, swindled into onerous contracts, unable to pay off their debts, one rather fictitious step above slaves. Every year, several die because they'd rather try walking away across the desert than live in those conditions. Nobody trusts anybody there. They're not going to help us find Harry unless it serves somebody's interests—somebody with pull."

Diamante returns to his seat, holding up the tracking map on his phone. "Harry's right *here*," he says, pointing out a building at the edge of a field of blue, the northern coast of Qumradhi.

"Is it a big building? Where is he inside?"

"It says it's sixty stories—where is he? No idea. I have to scan more when we get there."

"That's all that thing tells you?"

"It's just an app!" he protests and I realize how tired we all are. "I forgot I'd installed it until you reminded me. I'm surprised it works at all."

I nod, apologetic. "Okay, I hear you. We'll figure it out when we get there." The truth is, I've no idea how we're going to do that. I'm still trying to get us past the airport.

A moment later, a powerful-looking fellow in a flight suit climbs the stairs and prowls the aisle, eyeing the ID badges until he spots us. I read the glint of recognition in his eyes. He's alone and unarmed, as far as I can tell, but that doesn't stop every muscle in my body from tensing.

"If anything comes up," he says, "you're with the 3077th Air Wing; here's the contact." He offers a stiff business card with 3077th Air Wing insignia, lots of military acronyms that mean nothing to me and a phone number and promptly disappears below.

We exchange confused glances, trying not to be obvious.

And failing. An overly-fit-looking gent across the aisle, who's been pulling bottles of expensive wine from a case he's laid onto the adjacent seats, sees our predicament and leans our way. "The 3077th are our boys in Wadiirah. Big base on the mainland. We've spread the word all over the area that American contractors and soldiers are governed by UCMJ—" he waits to see if this registers. It does not. "Under the Uniform Code of Military Justice, you're guilty until proven innocent—we make damn sure the locals understand that. So when they meet a nasty American, they're happy to hand you over to the MP's, assuming you'll get your ass kicked."

"And what happens?"

"Are you with the 3077?"

"No."

"Then they've got no jurisdiction. They'll just ship you home," he says.

"No matter what?" Thinking back, it's a bad question, one that betrays my innocence (there's that *word* again). But he isn't thrown.

"Well, if you kill somebody, they'll be pissed, but—it's a loophole. Every system's got one, right? So that's us—we're the loophole." He winks at me, just like Harry would and goes back to watching the Kardashians on his iPad.

At first, the line just washes over me, like a good punchline should. And then, as I sink into my seat and take in the cabin, the whole scene transforms before my eyes, like petrol dissolving on a road washed with rain.

You'd know, if you woke up on this deck without explanation, that it isn't an airliner. There's no movie, though everyone seems to have brought iPads and headphones. The seats are too wide and the legroom too plentiful—you can actually sit like a human being—but the seats face the back of the plane, there's no portholes to look out of, no flight crew, no drinks and no food service. Our fellow travelers are dressed casually, but they're all ridiculously fit and keep to themselves. They virtually scream 'military' but there are no nametags here, no insignias. No one asks.

I'm the individual in Seat 57 and the crew knows where I'm going but not why or what I'm doing once we land—because no one's asked and no one will. My ID is bogus but nobody's checked it—and no one will.

We're the loophole...

I take a deep breath and truly relax, for the first time since I heard my name over the police headset.

I've spent fifteen years caught up in not getting caught, learning the rules of the game and how far I can bend them without having to pay for it. It's become second-nature.

Now, thanks to Dieter's magic pass, we've slipped over to the other side of the veil. I understand all at once how guys like him become guys like him. On his side of the divide, nobody pays for *anything*.

It's the same atmosphere that made me so uncomfortable when Hastings, Dieter and Mr. Woczynski walked into our office—*no* rules, no limits. A world that thinks rules are for the suckers who aren't on the plane.

I lean over to Sara. "Harry's reading the Bible. According to him, the Bible says Noah was a good man 'for his time'."

She looks as puzzled as I was when Harry brought it up. "That's nice—and?"

"Harry says this means God accepts relativity, moral relativity. We all live in context, in a time and a society—and can only be judged fairly within that context.

"For example, we're moving an iconic vintage race car onboard a Defense Department military transport—and it's by no means the least military thing on board. The palette leaking white powder would set off alarms in every airport in the civilized world—it's a cartoon of drug trafficking. The speedboat in the custom cradle is a Riva Aquarama, my guess is, late 60's, early 70's, handmade, mahogany, double inline motors, goes for about half a million at auction, on the rare occasions you can find one. Nobody's using it to fight the War on Terror—but here it is on the plane. The Humvee, next to the 917 in the cargo bay, *is* military hardware but there's something off about it. It's sitting awfully low on its springs—those things are built to carry ten men in full military gear without sinking an inch, so whatever it's carrying is very heavy indeed. Want to hazard a guess? Gold bricks, maybe? And this is just this one plane from this one airport carrying today's anonymous cargo.

"None of these guys are worried about getting caught. Why should they? The System's not trying to catch them—they *are* the System. They know what happens to people who play by the rules—and that's not going to happen to them.

"If they kill somebody in a foreign land, they get shipped safely home, care of the 3077th. If they want to smuggle opium, speedboats or one-of-a-kind racing cars, they're invisible to records, law and history, because there's always a loophole for whatever *they* want."

"We're not really in a position to complain, are we?" she says and she's got a point.

"I'm just saying I used to think Harry and I were mad pirates. Looking around here, I feel like a rank amateur. These guys made us look like chumps."

She doesn't quite get it and I guess there's no reason she should.

"I don't know if this is much of a defense but I'm just feeling kind of righteous at the moment. Maybe, for my time, being just a swindler makes me a relatively decent guy. I'll admit that's not a rigorous standard but I'll take it."

I can't tell if she's considering this idea or hating it.

"You still have your Bourne phone?"

She nods.

"Can I have it?" She hands it over. "My job," I say, punching in a number, "is to find the seam and push it open."

QUMRADHI

Qumrahdi, the capitol of Wadiirah, is designed to be seen from the porthole of a jetliner. The sun looks ten feet overhead and a hundred miles wide, glaring off a fever dream skyline of faceted, scalloped, pincered, twisted, Lego'd shapes in gimlet, azure and other brilliant shades, against the deep green of the Persian Gulf.

Things take a right turn—literally—as soon as we touch down. The plane pulls off the runway early, rolling to a hangar set as far as you can get from the passenger terminal.

Two Tech Sergeants come up the stairs, directly to our row. "You three, follow us, please," they say, in a tone that does not allow for objection. All my paranoia kicks in but I feel Sara's hand on my arm. She smiles and follows. By the time we hit the stairs, she leans into my ear and says, "Relax. There's two of them and three of us. They're not armed and they're not surrounding us." She's right—if they were arresting us, that's definitely how they would do it.

We exit into a blinding, broiling Middle East afternoon. The mouth of the plane is open; I see crew buzzing around the Porsche, rolling it carefully onto the runway. Two uniformed Wadiiran soldiers stand at the edges of the hangar door. As we approach, they snap to attention.

Inside the hangar stands Prince Rahim in his ceremonial white robe and *keffiyeh*—I don't think I've ever seen him in full regalia before, other than in pictures.

-You offered greetings to Prince Rahim, whom you've met at a ceremonial occasion, and went on your way. What happened next?

Hold up! What's your hurry?

-We can hear this part of the story from Prince Rahim.

The hell you can. I want my version on the record here and now.

`-Let's be clear—there is no 'record'. We`
`will decide what story will be told at the`
`end and that will be the record.`

Well, okay. Thanks for making that clear. I know where I stand now. Nonetheless, I'm still telling my story until you stop me.

Rahim's face is grave; any familiarity I've ever had with him suddenly feels perilously inappropriate. I nod respectfully and wait to be spoken to.

"I hope you had a safe journey," he says.

"Thank you. Our God was good to us."

He raises an eyebrow; a smile tugs at his lips. "I didn't know you had a God, Nicky." This is the Rahim I know and I'm so relieved he's shown up.

"Flying brings Him to the front of the line."

"Not just flying, I suspect," he says and waits for me to reply. I don't, so he continues. "I was surprised to hear from you."

"Well, I have your car! Le Mans winner, first Porsche to—"

"I know what it is. I'm very pleased about the car, of course. I'm merely surprised, with the Paris police searching for you, that your first thought is to bring me a gift. Or do I misunderstand?"

Coming from Rahim, the master of implication, this is a straight shot across the bow. Is *he* sending me back? Arresting me? I still see no guards nearby, other than the two at the gate.

I take a chance—to not answer directly. "Well, you misunderstand if you consider it a gift."

He smiles again, thank heavens.

"The Quran says, 'With Every Difficulty, there is Relief.' Relief is part of the process, but you must make room for it to occur. We spoke of a price a month or two ago and, as long as I am content with the car, it should not be a problem. I will admit I was disturbed when I heard you were heading here, concerned about the diplomatic ramifications—but when I was told you were arriving on a C5A, I realized there was more here than meets the eye."

Again, here's Dieter's veil protecting us, a system that doesn't want to know too much. "That's shrewd of you, as always," I say.

"And of you, I suspect. Clearly, you're protected— though by whom is not so clear at the moment." He stares at me—do I want to clear this up for him? I do not. "I'm willing to do my part. I have arranged a secure location for your discreet short-term use here—a gated community just outside the city, you'll have your own quarters and I'll provide open accounts at the local markets and pharmacies, you can call out for anything you need. Your host will be Colonel Qadir, one of my most trusted security men, from a fine family." You know Colonel Qadir, maybe?

    `-I am Colonel Qadir.`

Oh. Sorry about that. Rahim said your place was terrific. But clearly, no matter what he called it, it was still house arrest. And I couldn't do that—I had to find Harry.

    `-You were a guest. You should have`
`trusted us.`

Would you have let me out of the house?

    `-Of course not.`

Like I said, I had to find a way to worm out of this. "Um, that's very gracious, Rahim, however—"

He cuts me off with a look. "The Quran speaks of a guest's hospitality for three days—any more than that is charity bestowed upon him. And it says whoever believes in God and the Last Day, let him speak good words or else remain silent."

Which I took to mean, shut up and wait for another opportunity. "I understand your Highness has a watch you want me to sell?"

He brightens—we're onto business now, comfortable territory. "I do." He pulls a leather case from under his robes—they have pockets? "We need the best price and you know the sort of person who can help us."

I open the case and recognize the watch before he can say the name.

"A Rolex, a Reference 4113 Split-Second Chronograph."

He enunciates every syllable as though the name itself was worth big money. As well he might. This is one of those stories I know by heart. Rolex made twelve, as gifts for racing drivers in the 40's. Several have changed hands recently for anywhere from 800,000 to 1.6 million Swiss Francs. Watches are quoted in Swiss Francs because, naturally, that's where the crazy watch collector auctions are held.

"Any idea of the original owner?" One was meant for Ettore Bugatti. If it's that one...

"Alas, *non*. But it's genuine, with a letter of authenticity from the factory. And the original band—fawn leather."

Is Collecting an official diagnosis yet? Because surely it carries all the hallmarks of a major disease. Hallucinations, delusions and unwarranted euphoria. Extremely bad judgment with money, except for the hardnosed one per cent (like Rahim). Of course, my trade is locating and catering to the afflicted in all walks of life.

"The case looks a bit weathered—"

"—as though someone had driven several races wearing it." Rahim knows the game and plays it well. I hear his half-smile before I see it.

"You sure you don't want to keep it for yourself?"

"That would be inappropriate. It was the possession of a man who embezzled funds from his own business."

"So you took his million-franc wristwatch?"

"To reimburse the investors. He no longer has a wrist, so it is not really inconvenient for him."

"Oh God, Rahim, don't tell me that!" I moan, involuntarily, before the image is even fully digested.

"Tell you what?"

"'He no longer has a wrist...' You cut his hand off?"

"It is our law and custom."

"C'mon Rahim, you're a civilized person."

"We are a civilized nation."

"Sure—in between cutting people's limbs off."

"Uncivilized societies are lawless. Our law is ancient; our people know the punishment for bad behavior."

"You cut his hand off. Don't tell me that's a penal code."

"He met all the conditions. If he was insane or stole under duress, his hand would not be taken. If he stole from his own child or stole the looting of war, he would not lose a hand. If he returns the property before trial or it was stolen from a public place where it was not kept secure, the same thing. If what he stole was Haram—wine or pork—there is no penal action."

"So if he steals something he's not supposed to have in the first place, you suspend punishment. That makes no sense at all."

"It's outside the boundaries of our system, I suppose. Or possibly these things are simply not valuable to us. The

Quran says if the theft is of something not of substantial value, there may be punishment but not a cutting."

"It's totally arbitrary."

"If you think a Yemeni immigrant to Belgium is a danger to society, you arrest him and put him on trial, with lawyers and precedents and evidence presented before a jury. Innocent until proven guilty, you take pride in this. If the same person remained home in Yemen, you send a drone and blow him and everyone near him to the next world without warning. Guilty—and then dead—without process. All systems are arbitrary."

"And if the thief were a member of the royal family—?"

"That would not happen," his voice plays a darker melody now. There's a warning here, if I insist on following this line.

"Of course not; you wouldn't let it. But maybe someone with a connection to the family—?"

"Compensation would be made."

"But you wouldn't chop his hand off."

"Of course not. He might need it for diplomatic occasions, matters of state."

"And that isn't hypocritical?"

"If your plumber finds $100 under your cabinet and walks off with it—and you prosecute him—he'll go to jail for years, in a filthy facility where he'll be raped and schooled to be an advanced criminal. If he's a trader for Goldman Sachs, invests $650 million badly and disrupts the entire Western economy, destroying the security of millions, he will receive a bonus at the end of the quarter."

"Even *I* think that's hypocritical."

"On the contrary—it's why I keep my money with Goldman Sachs. Clearly, their investments are protected."

"Actually, it's not a bad argument for cutting hands off—you go to lunch with your new broker and—Oh! No hand! Maybe I'll let someone else invest the pension fund!"

"You see? It's practical."

"Makes it easy to pick out the undesirables at a distance."

"You do the same. They're your brown-skinned people."

"You've got a great gig, Rahim—rule the world while posing as one of the downtrodden brown people whenever it suits you."

"It's because we have a superior God."

He leads me out of the hangar. The C5A is in the distance, whining its way to the passenger terminal, having left behind the pristine Porsche 917K.

"Ahh—she is lovely. And fearsome." He walks around the car, checking each surface for imperfections, of which there are plenty.

"It's a 1970's race car, not a *Concours d'Elegance* model," I remind him.

"It is exactly the sort of symbol I'd hoped for," he smiles. He snaps a finger and two soldiers appear out of nowhere, somehow affixing a license plate to the rear of the car. WADIIONE, it reads. Just the thing for an anonymous joyride.

"She really should be seen by the public, with you driving," I suggest. Anything that might get me off the premises without going directly to house arrest.

He shrugs. "It's always a conflict; the needs of prestige versus the dignity of my position. Luckily, there are other members of the family who manage this conundrum more skillfully." He claps me on the shoulder and nods to Diamante. He takes Sara's hand and kisses it—she meets his eye boldly. "I have arranged an escort for you. Enjoy your stay for this brief period."

Meaning, *don't overstay your welcome.* Which really shouldn't be a problem. If we're not out of here in twenty-four hours, Rahim will be the least of our problems.

GRAND PRIX

-So let us now move on from Prince
Rahim.

You wish. He pops up again, as if you didn't know.

-I think you'd be far better off
answering questions—

—than making you nervous. Sure, no problem. I'll tell you what happened and, at the end, we'll see who has a better idea what Rahim wants to hear.

-That's *Prince* Rahim to you.

See? That's why I'm going to have the right answer and you won't.

Anyway, Rahim's disappeared, leaving us alone with a huge airport and a 917. And we hear the approach of rolling thunder.

It's a carnival of extravagant toys. A deep gray Lamborghini Aventador and a jade green convertible twin, three red Ferrari's, an XX, La Ferrari and a fantastic old Daytona, a naked-aluminum Bugatti Veyron, an old-school British Racing Green Aston Martin, two Maserati's and a silver Porsche Carrera GT, all of them revving their engines, the Aventador spitting flames just for fun. Roughly $25 million in investment cars, except these guys are driving them in broad daylight.

Sara says, "I feel under-dressed."

Doors open and five or six young men lift themselves out of the cars, two in the white robe/*keffiyeh* look, the others in an odd array of branded t-shirts and khakis, expensive sneakers and gold chains. Geek gangstas with money.

The Bugatti pulls to the front, polished-aluminum front end blinding in the desert sun, the reflection nearly blotting out the red-and-black painted rear end of the car. The door pops straight up and some sort of deafening Middle-Eastern hip-hop bellows from inside—tabla, congas, oud, electronic percussion and a bass note to stop your heart.

And rising up out of the car is Rahim's brother Yusuf.

"Yo Dog, whattup?"

If Rahim is the heart of the royal family, Yusuf is its acid reflux. He is maybe twenty-three, with the big eyes and narrow chin of a child, dressed in a black-and-red Manchester United jersey, workout pants, a pair of limited-edition Jordan's I could resell in Japan for a couple thou if they aren't too worn and a watch that redefines the limits of bling.

"What's with the watch, Yusuf?"

"Seeeeriously, dog!" Yusuf lifts it to give me the full-on view. There's a huge logo, smack in the middle, that I don't recognize. The case, however, requires pumping iron just to raise to eye-height. Yusuf swings it up and down like a barbell, biceps popping. "Car—watch—car—watch?" The logo says...B?

"Bugatti makes watches?"

"It's dope, my brother, just like this car you've brought me!" he says, eyeing the 917 hungrily.

-You gave Prince Rahim's 917 to Prince Yusuf?

Why? You have a problem with Prince Yusuf?

-Of course not. Prince Yusuf is an
invaluable member of the ruling family. I
just thought—

You thought he'd crash it the first ten seconds in the driver's seat—so did I. No, of course, I didn't give it to him. If a two-year-old wants nitroglycerine, he's at least going to have to arm-wrestle me for it.

"*Rahim's* car," I reply, as casually as I can.

"Yeah yeah, it's his, of course," Yusuf sputters. "But he won't mind, once I drop you off." *To House Arrest*—now that it's me against Yusuf, that ain't happening. By the way, why didn't *you* come to escort me?

-I was in a conference on the mainland.
I could not return in time—

And of all the people in the world to replace you, Rahim—who's no fool—picked Yusuf? Just chew on that one for a while.

Yusuf pulls a slip of paper from his pocket and lets it flutter in the breeze. "You're getting kind of common, Nicky. Cheque made to 'Cash'?"

"I'm just a man of the people," I smile, snatching it out of his hand before he can drop it. Which he would, just for kicks. I've made a few bucks off of Yusuf but never without more trouble than it's worth.

So then he starts to vlog.

-To—I'm sorry?

You haven't seen Yusuf's vlog's? You're probably not his demographic. He's the video blog king of the Middle East. A new episode posts nearly every day, heavily watched all around the region, doing major social media PR for the kingdom. Yusuf's posse figure heavily in most episodes, trading in one supercar for another, zooming around the highways in packs, bouncing dune buggies over the beach and shopping for all kinds of insanely-priced, limited-edition bling.

Most of his homeboys live with their parents in what look to Westerners like middle-class homes, concrete boxes with a carport and a little garden on the side, nothing fancy—but with a couple of Lamborgini's in the driveway, a separate room for the video game consoles, the 4K television with the seven-way speakers and VR headset and they stay up all night once a year for Apple Day, the rollout of the new line, taking in the hype and paying through the nose to glom the best and latest models as soon as they're released.

Wadiirah pays its citizens for being citizens and Yusuf is their aspirational role model.

His Vlog is an online campaign of self-love and consumerism, reminding outsiders how great Wadiirah is and reminding Wadiiran homeboys how envied they are by everyone else.

-Why should we not be proud of our system?

Sure, why not? There hasn't been a revolution yet and surely that is the point.

-There will never be a revolution here.

Not as long as the money holds out.

Yusuf pulls his phone out and starts zipping around the 917, inches from the surface, sharing his new toy online and inspecting it far more closely than Rahim did. He's smitten, as any little boy would be.

In that infatuation, I see opportunity.

I help Diamante pull the portable starter into position. "Exactly how do I drive from here to Harry's hotel?" I ask him.

On the mapping program, thankfully, it's a simple trip—eleven miles away, fourth exit off the freeway leading directly to the waterfront development.

Diamante attaches the starter. I switch on the two fuel pumps, work the choke, pump the throttle and hit the black starter button. The thing coughs, coughs again, spouts grey smoke and, thank you, turns over. LOUD! She's a race car, twelve cylinders, no muffler, no pollution control, no restraint. I pop the throttle a couple times and she blasts a throaty roar, overwhelming the garden-variety Ferraris and Bugattis with their metallic paint and boytoy airbags. SAFETY equipment? We don't need no stinkin' safety equipment!

Yusuf swells to double his normal height. "Whoa, let me *at* her, dog!! I can't wait to drop the hammer!"

Now, at this point, I should mention that Yusuf has appeared out of the *passenger* seat of his Bugatti. Amani, his sister, appears now out of the driver seat.

Amani is sharp as a knife, funny and lovely, beautiful shape, hair and make-up (she gives lessons on her own vlog three times a week). She's got this half-smile, the boys call her the Qumrahdi Mona Lisa. If you've got a feminist wife (like me, for the moment), you recognize that face and sense of humor, a world-weary combination of strained tolerance and condescension. It can't be easy being the woman in this boy-gang.

Yusuf has the fanciest, fastest cars going but contents himself shooting the vlog and talking trash while his sister does the driving. That's also made Amani a feminist icon (something no one would dare call her out loud) in the Arab world. It's wonderful and incongruous, as a Westerner, to watch her, knowing that, twenty minutes away (ten for her), women aren't allowed to drive at all. She's a visible counter-argument to that world and Wadiirah's PR cabal have cannily unleashed her on Yusuf's vlog without ever openly promoting her or even admitting she exists. A woman driving is only low-profile if no one mentions it so no one does—but that doesn't make her one bit less subversive. Amani's online appearances are yet another reason for her neighbors to hate Wadiirah.

-I will point out that we have cordial relationships with all our neighbors.

Okay, so we both feel the need to put things 'on the record' here.

-I don't know what you're talking about.

Anyway, there is a gap in both sibling's motoring education—and I know what it is.

"Amani doesn't drive a stick, does she?" I ask Yusuf innocently, already knowing the answer—they're both too young to have ever needed to master a clutch. "Do you?"

"I've seen them," he says. "How hard can it be?" But he knows better. The clutch is the downfall of shallow drivers everywhere. Crestfallen suddenly, he's a boy who can't take home the puppy until it gets its shots. Yusuf really is about nine or ten in grown-up years. He's never had a desire denied or a goal beyond the mall, the car dealer or the Apple Store. Until now.

"It's not a problem," I tell him, visualizing the map on Diamante's phone. "I'm hungry. Let's air her out, blast on over someplace for lunch. You can see how she runs, shoot some video for the blog, then you get yourself a couple clutch lessons and you'll be good to go. Sara, why don't you ride with Amani—I assume Yusuf wants the passenger seat?"

"Hell yeah, I want the passenger seat!" he says and fastens himself onto the shelf next to the driver's bucket.

I let out the clutch, the 917 jumps forward and we roll toward the airport gate, popping the throttle just enough to keep her from stalling. Yusuf raises his door and waves at the guards.

As the pylon begins to rise, I see our *real* escort—four police speedsters, a pair of Lamborghini's and a pair of Bugatti's, with flashing lights and sirens on top, the cherries on a sundae. They swiftly race down to the eight-lane expressway below, two cars stopping traffic behind us and two racing ahead, moving the plebes out of the two left lanes, giving us room.

Room to race. I've seen enough of Yusuf's vlogs to know that's what's about to happen.

The bar rises out of sight. I put my foot down and the 917 takes off. I didn't think to ask Larry for earplugs and this mother is LOUD! Not to mention, with the lack of air conditioning (RACING CAR), fixed windows (ditto) and the outside heat (how's 114°F strike you? Thank God, it's December!), it's a broiler inside.

Surrounded by million-dollar cars fifty years newer, the glory of 21st Century computer design, we are *just* maintaining our lead. Yusuf pumps his fist against the tiny plastic side windows as the world's most entitled kids give chase, determined to pass and show up this 1970 museum piece.

In the meantime—omigod, this *is* a race car. The road looks glass-smooth but the car's scrabbling about, following invisible grooves and imperfections in the roadbed. The engine is lumpy, out-of-time, the steering heavy as concrete. Every tiny kink in what looked like a straight road is now a major turn, requiring careful setup and throttle manipulation (which, so far, seems well-nigh impossible). The space-frame chassis (tubes filled with gas so the engineers could check mid-race to see if they'd cracked) is flexing like it's made of rubber. It's all I can do to stay on the road, much less compete with Amani driving the 917's domesticated great-grandchild.

And of course, she's the closest contender. The only reason Yusuf's lived down his sister being faster than him is that she beats his friends just as handily. Her Veyron actually has a higher top speed than the 917 but somehow I'm maintaining my tiny lead. To validate Prince Rahim's purchase, I can't let her catch me.

This is, after all, maybe the most fabled racing car of all. It damn well better beat his niece.

All at once, I remember a documentary I watched a few years ago, around the time of the first client request for a 917. One of the race drivers remembered Porsche's chief engineer telling him the throttle only had two settings—all the way up or all the way down, foot up or to the floor.

"Wave to your sister!" I scream at Yusuf.

"What?"

"WAVE TO YOUR SISTER! SHOW HER THE CAMERA!"

Yusuf waves, lens pressed to the window and Amani lets off the gas just a tiny bit, just reactively, to wave back politely, like the supportive (and photogenic) sister she is. In the split-second she does, I mash the pedal to the floor. Already doing about 140, the twelve-cylinder engine screams like a chorus of banshees, the car squirms a bit, settles on her haunches and leaps forward, gaining speed at a dizzying rate. "HOOOO-EEEE!!!" Yusuf revs his arms across the window. I can *hear* him—how fucking loud can this kid yell?

The frame still squirms but suddenly the car is planted on the road and the acceleration is Wile E Coyote-like. I may not hear again for a week and it don't bother me—this is

FUN! We pull handily away from the Bugatti and the rest of the crowd. I hold my advantage just long enough to make it official, then throttle back to a mere 130. I can now afford to let Amani catch me, successfully having obscured the fact that she would have eventually anyway.

And just ahead, I see the towers to the right of the highway—two dark copper scimitar-shaped skyscrapers curving toward each other, with a gleaming gold center section joining the two somewhere around the thirtieth floor. I coast into the sweeping exit ramp and the caravan follows.

"What're you doing, dog? We're supposed to go to Colonel Qadir's!"

"I want lunch. There's a good place here—I read about it on the plane."

"There are lots of good places. I got to deliver you. Rahim said—"

"Did he tell you about my situation?" I yell, watching Yusuf's reaction carefully.

-Are you sure you want this conversation on the record?

You said there was no record—I'm just telling my story the way it happened.

Yusuf puffs up while his cheeks go red, dying to boast about something he's not supposed to know. "You brought the bomb to Paris!" he bursts. He's *excited* about it!

"Rahim met Arafat once," he continues. "All they did was eat lunch. But they picked him up in a convoy and blindfolded him, like ten guys with Kalashnikovs, y'dig? And they drove him around Beirut for an hour to make sure nobody was following them and then he finds himself in the room with Arafat and twenty guards. They have hummus—not even good hummus—talk for twenty minutes and have a picture taken and Rahim's set for life! Nobody can diss him, dog, y'know? He's not a checkbook prince anymore! I'm never going to meet Arafat but I'm gonna deliver *you*!"

"You're a believer in terrorism?"

-I would be very careful here.

Please—we're talking about *Yusuf!* He defers for just a moment. "Not really—no offense—but it's solidarity, dog! I am *so* gonna get *laid*!"

It's weird, moments where the long pendulum of history is poised to swing one direction or the other come in the oddest giftwrap. RULE THREE: TELL THEM WHAT

THEY WANT TO HEAR. What does Yusuf really want to hear?

"That's why I'm so glad *you* showed up," I tell him, screaming precise enunciation over the engine roar. "*You can help me so much more than Rahim.*"

To say the kid's eyes light up is a gross understatement. He's been waiting to hear those exact words his entire life.

"I just can't disappear, not yet, Yusuf. When it's time, I'll go quietly—but right now, *I'm on a mission.*"

If the car was foreplay, we're now into heavy petting. A *mission*!

"Your phone's off, right?" I arch an eyebrow and he skitters like a pinball turning it off. "Take out the battery. They have ways of turning it on remotely, without you knowing," I confide and the kid nearly oozes out of his seat. Battery removed, I continue. "Rahim is as reliable a friend as I could ask for but he's…a bit conventional, know what I mean? I need someone *bold* to help me. Someone who…thinks outside the box! Colors outside the lines!" Yes, they're cliches. I've had three hours sleep in the last three days. I'm fucking *exhausted.*

"What can I do?" Yusuf asks.

"An important operative of mine is here in Qumrahdi—to put it plainly, he's been kidnapped here."

Yusuf's face goes dark. "That's no good, dog. No kidnappings allowed here except by the police. And then only—"

"—the unprotected, I bet."

"Exactly."

"But once in a while, just randomly, something slips by, maybe?"

"I don't think so. We're pretty strict about that."

A new thought pops into my head. "Is it worse or better to kidnap infidels? Is there a special punishment for that?" He stares into space. "You don't *know*?"

"You know all the French punishments?"

"You guys cut things *off*! If the French did that, I'd know the penal code by heart!"

"Well, this is disturbing," he admits.

"That's why I need you!" I say. "We have a pretty good idea where he is—but we have to get him out ourselves, without the police, without Rahim. The whole idea is to *protect* Rahim, not involve him. Besides, Rahim wouldn't know how to help us—he does everything by the book. But you? You're an *outlaw!*"

I know my princes. Yusuf sucks up this smoke so deeply, his eyes begin to water.

-You could have confided in Ah—uh, Prince Rahim—in the first place.

Sure. He controls the kingdom, he could surely have located the kidnappers eventually, couldn't he?

But again, remember our history, Harry's and mine. I don't know who's got Harry or why. I'm not sure what *else* we're going to find when we get there. Maybe an angry Wadiiran ex-customer, maybe someone in the royal family he'd feel obligated to favor.

-We don't have such problems with the royal family.

Or maybe we did something ourselves— unintentionally, of course—that had unpleasant repercussions after we pulled out. I'm not going to pretend that's never happened.

And—if I'm being entirely transparent, which is what you want—

-Probably.

—well then, I don't trust Rahim because he's too smart, too shrewd and too subtle by half for me. If we truly offended him, he could disappear us without a mote of dust in evidence. Whereas, I'm pretty confident I can outplay Yusuf to the last move. At the moment, that's the only angle we've got, so I'm playing it for all it's worth.

"What I need for the next hour," I tell him, "is for you to be a spoiled, entitled Master of the Universe. I need you to throw your weight around to the point that people don't question, don't dare argue. I need a self-centered dick who knows the world exists to give him whatever he wants—until he wants something else, two minutes later."

Yusuf's eyes gleam like marbles.

"I won't even have to raise my voice," he says.

REAL ESTATE

The hotel complex sits on an island in a lagoon scooped out of the northern coast of Qumrahdi. Our garish caravan circles a courtyard of deep pink marble and onyx flagstone, engines revving like a swarm of gigantic bees. A mall bustles at ground level while four stories of garages, including a high-security, climate-controlled block for the most valuable cars, sit below-ground. This is where Diamante has leased a space for the 917.

Management sends out a flunky in a chic suit, either to quiet down the roar of our convoy or make us pay for the privilege. I recognize his officious look, the one that assumes *You all want to help me help you, now don't you?*

Yusuf rises from the passenger seat of the 917 and Flunky goes weak in the knees.

It's the family face. The whole royal family—father, two brothers, five sons and thirty-five cousins—all look a whole lot like each other and there's a portrait of one or two of them—the King, the Crown Prince, Prince Rahim (the Chief of Staff Prince), the Prime Minister Prince, the Junior Transport Minister Prince and sometimes the Commissioner of Housing Prince, thirty-five feet tall, on every other block and every other billboard all over Qumrahdi. The family face is branded on the national consciousness like Mickey Mouse, Colonel Sanders or Elvis.

Yusuf's got the family face and Flunky, confronted by this royalist nightmare, stops dead in his tracks.

"A secure garage has been arranged for this car, the property of Prince Rahim!" Yusuf proclaims.

Flunky checks his iPad. "We have nothing on our records—"

"It's under my name, 'Nicholas Marsh'," I explain. "A gift to the Prince from an old friend."

"A token of appreciation," Yusuf lays it on thick, making sure everyone understands he's an emissary of

Rahim. Driving Rahim's car! Sitting in the passenger seat, at least.

"Partition 27!" Flunky calls to the attendants, who appear from nowhere and push the 917 into the elevator (!) to the car penthouse below.

"We require at least one floor, possibly two or three, of your hotel," Yusuf continues, "where the feng shui is positive. I must sign off on the location personally. These are *spiritual* goals at work here—you see me, son?"

Flunky might be a little shaky, feng shui-speaking, but he understands hierarchy. He nods staccato and backs into the lobby, promising Yusuf the best of everything.

Yusuf's sidekick Hassan—I know him from the vlogs—arranges parking for the posse while Diamante works his way across the front of the building, feigning glamor shots of the cars while monitoring Harry's phone signal.

"He's a way's up."

"Middle? High? Which wing?"

"Can't tell."

"That's no good. We can't search all those floors."

"Whoever's kidnapped him," Sara injects, reading from her phone, "is not stupid. This place has twenty-five elevators, each one programmed for specific floors only. The elevator doors won't open unless your key has the right access."

Yusuf pops over.

"Sara!" I say. "Yusuf was impressed that Rahim got to meet Arafat. How many times did you interview Arafat?"

She grimaces. "Three. Ask me how often he told me something worth writing."

Yusuf's eyes glaze over and he does what men have done to women like Sara for ten thousand years—he changes the subject.

"Where's your friend?"

"We're trying to get readings on our homing device."

"Looks like a phone."

"Doesn't it? They're clever that way. Anyhow, we're not getting clear info so far. He's up there but we don't know how far or which side of the building."

"You need more detail."

"Tell me about it," I grumble and his face sets, as though I've just given him really serious instructions.

The lobby is a jumble of glass and gold plate. You could get lost in the reflections. Flunky approaches Yusuf as we sweep inside. "I've reserved the entire twenty-third floor for your party," he offers. In three minutes, his body language has morphed from arrogant snot to *I-live-to-suffer-for-you.*

Yusuf pulls him up short.

"Did I *choose* the twenty-third floor?" Yusuf whispers and Flunky nearly shrivels into the corner. The threat in Yusuf's voice is the terrifying self-assurance of someone who *knows* he will get exactly what he wants. "You *did* hear me say I would choose?"

"Yes, Your Highness."

"So I will choose—the floor or floors—in due time. For now, we go to the Skylounge."

He points upward, to the fancy smoked-glass bubble lounge straddling the two towers. Flunky's skin passes quickly from suntan-umber to stroke-green.

"The—the Skylounge is reserved for a corporate affair," he sputters.

Yusuf just stares. No retort, no words, no change of expression, no blinking, no letup. It's amazing how quickly this becomes unendurable, even for me just watching. Flunky attempts a response but it ends in a strangled squeak.

"We go to the Skylounge," Yusuf repeats, in exactly the same tone of voice and Flunky trots to corral elevators for our party of twelve.

~~~

As we walk to the lifts, Yusuf tells Diamante, "Read your meter as we go up. If you can narrow the strongest signal to three floors, I'll find your man." He flashes me his on-camera smile. "I've got that app," he offers. "Great for locating stray girlfriends."

Yesterday, I wouldn't have taken Yusuf's word if he said cancer was bad for me. Now he's making suggestions and we're taking them. When you're standing on the Pole, everything looks like a compass.

We're so close to Harry now. *Find out where he is, figure out how to get inside, figure out how to get him out.* This trip is a Russian nesting doll of troubles.

Diamante stations himself near the control panel, so he can read his app and the floor display at a glance. The smoked-glass cupola bobs upward like a cork, the skyline rearranging itself, fountains, construction cranes and licorice-stick towers preening as we rise.

The Skylounge is packed. The corporate party is raging, a mixed group from the Godzilla of Wall Street banks kicking back against a wall of tinted windows, the Saudi industrial seascape to the North merging into Qumrahdi's skyline and the endless Gulf stretching eastward unto infinity. Flunky has a word with the bank managers and Yusuf joins in, emphasizing the royal nature of our intrusion on their bar. Three minutes later, attendants drag a rolling partition through the center of the room, separating the two parties. Hassan coordinates the drink order while food appears on shiny stainless-steel carts.

Yusuf huddles with us, soaking up the spy game. "So what do we know?"

Diamante looks conflicted. "The signal was at its strongest just before we stopped. So he might be right below us."

"But you're not sure."

"Sure? No. Let me do some more readings."

Yusuf's posse have spread onto the window seats, drinks are flowing and the aisles are clogged with showcases on rolling carts—watches, cellphones, videogame consoles, fancy laptops, 4K televisions in multi-monitor displays. And suddenly we're swarming in women—tall, mostly blond and, from their accents, Eastern European. Everything has its price and these guys are the market.

-Is this relevant to—?

I told you before—it's *my* story. You need to know what I would say in court.

-You will never appear in court.

Maybe not *here*. I'm an American citizen. Maybe I'd rather be tried in the US.

-We have influence. You could get a long sentence.

They don't cut shit *off* though, do they?

So Diamante wanders absent-mindedly into the center of the room, reading signal strength but it's bad timing. Hassan rises off the couch to meet him and I can read the ominous look in his eyes. I reach them just before Hassan's outstretched hand can slap the phone from Diamante's.

"Hold on, brother," I say. "Everything's cool."

"NO phones," Hassan says. Diamante is shaken, letting me take the lead. I hold his phone up to Hassan's face, showing him the most recent photos Diamante took — Paris street scenes, a computer screen shot and one of the flight deck of the C5A. Nothing from tonight.

"No pictures," I tell him. "We're measuring emissions for everyone's safety, okay? We're friends to Prince Yusuf — and the family." I lean on the last few words and watch him stand down from alert.

"What the hell was that?" Diamante asks, after we're back at our table.

Yusuf shakes his head. "Pictures are dangerous."

"Pictures of what?"

"Booze," Yusuf explains. "Women. They love we've got the cars, the watches, the computers and the jets. But somehow we're supposed to sit home with the wife and six kids and pray five times a day."

"Who's 'they'?" Sara asks, returning with Amina from the end of the bar, where they have been conferring and sheltering themselves from the rabid boys.

"Them!" he points, out the window and down, where presumably the little people are surviving the 114°

sandblasting outside. "They know—we all know—what's going on. But you don't poke the bear, y'know? Where's your friend?"

Diamante checks his latest readings. "Not below us," he says. "His signal's coming from above."

"Isn't *this* the top floor?"

Diamante shrugs. "They've stuffed him in a crawl space? Or it's a repeater and he's back in Paris somewhere? All I know is, the signal's up there."

The posse is rapidly getting trashed and pairings of both sexes are getting serious. Sara points out one boy-on-boy couple pulling the curtain on a private alcove.

-This is not relevant or necessary.

That's what Sara said! "Isn't that worth a beheading around here?" she asks cheerfully.

"Not up *here*," Amina says but everyone seems to want to bury the subject. Just like you.

"Time to make progress, isn't it?" says Yusuf and I'm pleased to hear it. Kidnappers have deadlines. We've waited too long for Harry's safety as it is.

Yusuf steps into the center of the room and Flunky appears instantly. Yusuf's soft-spoken voice again registers as barely-repressed sadism.

"Am I mistaken?" he asks. "Were we not told *this* is the top floor?"

"It is the top r-re-regular floor!" Flunky answers, tripping over 'regular' in his desperate attempt to slide it past unnoticed.

"So what's above? Something *irregular*?"

"The penthouse!" Flunky panics. "It's occupied!"

"Good. We will go there, with my friends."

"I—I have to get approval from the desk," Flunky says, pulling his phone from his pocket. Yusuf grabs it calmly and smashes it on the floor.

"Your phone isn't working," he smiles. "You can get approval later." Flunky leads the way toward the elevator bank.

Yusuf smiles at me. "Dog, it's gotta be time to call Rahim, right? We know where your friend is, so now it's the tactical squad."

"We *don't* know," I squirm. "Not for sure."

"Whoever heard of kidnappers taking the penthouse?" Sara asks. "It would look bad if the tactical squad burst in on honeymooners from Amsterdam, wouldn't it?"

"We'll go up with the hotel guy," I offer. "You can stay here—"

"Oh hell no," Yusuf chirps and didn't I know that was coming. I can sense self-destructive pride at half a mile's distance—it must feel familiar. "If there's danger, I'm your man." His bodyguard appears at his shoulder again—at least, he'll be more protected than the rest of us.

"I'm going too," Amina says.

"No, you should stay—" Yusuf makes the attempt, to no avail.

"Brother, you may need me to explain this to Rahim," she replies and Yusuf goes dead silent.

I sigh. "Let's scope the place out as quietly as we can."

We watch the elevator pod rising up the tube toward us. When it arrives, three waiters emerge, in smart white jackets pushing serving carts.

"One moment, please," I say. Yusuf smiles and they obey. A minute later, Diamante and Sara and I are wearing their jackets, more or less, pushing their carts and carrying unopened bottles of champagne as Flunky turns the key to get the lift up that one extra invisible floor.

And then things start to happen way too fast.

The doors open in a tiny landing. The penthouse door is modern, monolithic and rather threatening-looking. A small CCTV camera stares its red eye at us.

Flunky is about to knock. That's when I realize what a dangerous stupid situation I've put us all in.

Harry could be tied to a chair, tied to a bomb, surrounded by men with automatic weapons. Held in peril by an angry corporation head we swindled or the very well-off husband of some poorly-judged victim. All the negative possibilities form an impressive stack in my mind.

"You should stand behind your bodyguard," I tell Yusuf.

"I don't have bodyguards," he answers. He glances at the Muscle Beach refugee behind him. "That's Cousin Mahmood," he says. "He lifts."

"Stand behind him anyway," I hiss and motion the same message to Sara and Amina. Amina complies. Sara, predictably, does not.

"In your dreams," Sara says, jostling her cart up even with mine.

"Don't knock—just unlock the door," I tell Flunky while squeezing out a prayer to an unfamiliar God. Flunky glances at Yusuf, who nods from behind Cousin Mahmood, who doesn't look thrilled about having suddenly become a human shield.

Flunky pulls open the door with a sudden whoosh and blinding light—the setting sun skimming over the Gulf.

"You have the honor—" he pronounces "—of a visitation—"

"Room Service!" I call, shoving my cart and Sara's in through the door. If there are guns inside, let's give them a target.

The carts clatter across the shiny floor and slam together at the edge of the sunken living room. One cart tips a wheel over the edge, teeters and finally commits, crashing down in a cacophony of shattered glasses and plates.

Deep shadows move across a vista of white leather and Expressionist murals. Clouds track shadows across the waves below. Not a sound, so far, no reaction whatever.

Flunky, protected by the weight of his self-importance, marches into the center of the firing range. "Congratulations! You are to receive a great honor, a visitation by the Prince—"

Okay, no gunshots, no noise.

Also, no food (other than our trays), no clothes, no magazines, no signs of habitation other than a few lights burning electricity.

"Hello?" Flunky says, all uncertainty. "Hello?"

"Harry?" Diamante calls. "*Jevo?*"

"Come out, come out, wherever you are," Sara moans, motioning us toward the bedroom door. Toward the moving shadows *under* the door, to be specific.

I grab a taper from the gas fireplace; cousin Mahmood pulls a cricket bat from a corner. We station ourselves silently on either side of the door. Yusuf and Amani duck behind the wet bar. Flunky remains frozen in place, as though he's grown roots in the center of the suite.

We hear rustling inside and then the door opens, revealing the quizzical figure of Harry Sandler, squinting into the light, in silk pajamas and fuzzy slippers.

THE REVEAL

Harry's first move, emerging from his bedroom cocoon, is sheer instinct—he heard Diamante's voice and responded. His second—taken by surprise, taking us, and the upended lunch carts, in all at once—is confusion.

"Oh hello!" he says. "Did I order? *What* did I order, I suppose that's the proper question, isn't it?" He offers this with a brightness intended to obscure the fact that he's got no idea who we are.

He pulls a cloth napkin off the remaining upright cart and tucks it into the neck of his dressing gown but I can see the gears turning. He doesn't remember ordering a meal and some part of him is wondering if several of us don't look familiar.

I tuck around him into the bedroom and then the bath. There has to be someone else here, surely—but there isn't.

He's wandering the living room, pretending to search for something. He senses something's off—there are too many of us for room service and don't some of us ring a bell? Are the others—Yusuf, Flunky—familiar at all? He gives Amina a long appraising look. He's trying to put solid ground under his feet but, so far, no luck.

He lifts the lids on the trays, pointedly ignoring the mess of the upended cart. Did he order sandwiches and beer—for cronies and insiders—or champagne and duck pate—for potential clients? Does he even remember what he does for a living?

"Harry? Harry?" Diamante comes to embrace him but Harry pulls back; he actually flinches at the approach. Pain is all over Diamante's face, mingled with a new fear—he doesn't know this man who agonizingly doesn't know him. Harry peers at his face, acknowledging the voice calling his name—it's something but not much. Diamante is shattered.

"What are you doing here, Harry?" I ask.

"Having a fine time, I must say. Finest weather in the world. Don't you love it?" He knows he knows me, he's trying to place me, the name is so close and if he gets one syllable, it'll all come back. In the meantime, he's hedging, accepting wobbly as the preferred alternative to complete collapse. "Coming from a rainy country, I crave the sunshine, automatically feels like a holiday."

"This is who we were looking for," I turn to Yusuf, gesturing toward the elevators. "We're great now, thanks."

But Yusuf's not concerned with how *we* are. His eyes are wide, his expression alarming—a pot boiling over. And then he jumps at Harry.

"You're *not* Harry Sandler!" he growls, grabbing him by the collar and throwing him against the wall. Harry goes down like a plywood shed hit by a runaway train. "I don't remember your real name but I know that face! Your picture's been on our wall as long as I remember, so we never forget! Uncle Khalil and the Greek pots!"

"Yusuf!" Amina yells. Harry's got that pigeon-face I've seen so often recently, the one that vaguely recalls disaster but not exactly how he brought it on. Mahmood grabs Yusuf and pulls him to a safe distance.

And now I'm defensively trying to reconstruct how I ended up in charge of all contact with the Wadiiran royal family. Did I take that initiative or did Harry 'suggest' it to me? I can't remember but I could probably make a good guess.

"Oh my goodness, yes, I'd forgotten. How is Khalil?" Harry asks as though discussing an old friend, because that's how Harry regards people he's swindled—they've done him, after all, a wonderful service.

"He's dead a long time," Yusuf says, "but he can still be avenged." If there was a sword nearby, Harry's head would be rolling around the floor.

"Yusuf, don't be a fool," Amina kicks him.

"I'm so pleased everyone's satisfied," Flunky says, backing toward the elevator.

"I'm calling the police," Yusuf says, pulling his phone.

"Give me the phone," Diamante says, brandishing a dull-gray Glock in Yusuf's face. "Yours, too," he tells Flunky and cousin Mahmood, who hand them over. "Have a seat over there," motioning them onto the couches along the windows.

He sees my surprise. "It was a military transport. You didn't think they had guns? You too," he adds, to Amina, but Sara appears out of the bedroom and says, "She's okay, I'll be responsible for her." Diamante shrugs and lets it go.

"I suspect this is the laptop you wanted?" Sara says, handing it to me—and eyeing Diamante. "He's holding a gun on a member of the royal family—tell me this is part of your plan." Her forehead furrows in a way I find ludicrously attractive. "Tell me you *have* a plan."

"As soon as I do, I'll let you know," I answer and she sinks onto a chair next to Harry, groaning "God in heaven." I didn't know she was religious.

The sun has sunk below the horizon now, lights flickering on along the coast, headlights along the highway. I return to the task of reviving Harry Sandler or whoever is inside his body at the moment.

"Harry? Do you know who I am?"

Harry's eyeglasses perch on the bridge of his nose—he peers over them, quizzical.

"You're…" he starts, with a child's tone of voice. Then he takes another look at Diamante and, in a moment, the mists part.

"My love!" he exclaims and pivots back to Sara and me. "And you two! How disappointing! I pay Rene

Baudelaire good money to keep you on ice and here you are anyway."

"What the fuck are you doing here?"

"Why did you have us kidnapped?" Sara asks and *that*, he hears immediately.

"It's part of my plan, dearest."

"He has a plan," Sara mutters. I would kick her but she'd see it coming.

"I set a dinner date with her," Harry turns to me, "and texted you to come to my apartment, very important, so you'd be there for Rene." A text I didn't receive because my phone got stolen—but I showed up on time anyway. Perfect. "That's my plan—Rene's supposed to be keeping you busy."

"Forget Rene! What about the shipping certificate you signed my name to?"

"I did?"

"You don't remember?"

"Not at the moment." He makes a show of peeking around the end of the bar. "Not yet," he adds, as though it's a joke.

"We're supposed to be shipping a full container; marked as 'construction equipment' but—"

"But it's a bomb!" His face lights up. It's like turning on a radio—all of a sudden, he's Harry again!

The air goes out of me. It's like being punched.

"A big one!" he continues.

I'd assumed this part was a lie, that Harry didn't know, or at worst, that he'd been forced. I'd considered every possibility but this one.

"I planned it myself," he says, swelling with pride.

"You smuggled a bomb into Paris—and hung it on me?"

His face goes long and white, some sort of elongated pucker. "What are you talking about?" he says. "Paris? Why would I bomb *Paris*?"

"You just said—"

He stomps to the long northern wall of windows and sticks out a finger. "I'm smuggling a bomb into Ras Tanura! Right over *there*!"

The room goes dead silent. I need more something but I'm not sure what. "Huh?" is all that comes out of my mouth.

Sara's says, "The pipeline, Harry? You mean the pipeline?"

Harry's smile goes ear to ear. He nods like a child offered ice cream.

Sara's voice plays an undertaker's note. "The pipeline carries oil from all over the Arabian Peninsula to Ras Tanura, thirty miles north of here, where it's pumped into ships for transport around the world." Her face darkens. "What goes through there? Thirty million barrels a day?"

"Fifty!" Harry says.

I'm trying to make sense of this. "And you're going to blow it up? Like that'd stop the oil for—what? A week? Two?"

Harry rises in carnival dance, swaying to a tune I don't hear. "Oh no, no no no," he sings. "You're missing the beauty of the thing. I have a nuke."

Sara and I gasp like twins at the circus. "A *what*?"

"Remember the Armenian gentleman, Djermajian, last spring?"

"Anatole Djermajian, nutty even by our standards," I explain.

"The one who wanted to buy the Mona Lisa?"

"The one in the Louvre?" Sara snarks.

"No, the *real* one."

"Excuse me?"

"The Mona Lisa was stolen from the Louvre in 1911," Harry rises, winding up his tongue and letting go, as usual. "Greatest art theft of the Twentieth Century. Vincenzo Peruggia, former Louvre employee, walks in one morning with the workers, wearing the uniform white smock, lifts the painting and walks out with it under the smock when the Louvre closes the next evening. Hangs it in his bedroom, same as Napoleon, for three years while the world goes crazy looking for it. Only gets caught because he's patriotic and decides to return it to Italy—"

"—who didn't own it anyway," I interject. "Djermajian, though, was convinced Peruggia made himself a copy and returned *that* one, while stashing the real Mona Lisa in some hillside village—"

"Vietri Sul Mare."

"Right. And I told him that, if the real Mona Lisa was still out there, he couldn't afford it. So?"

"Well, it turns out he could!" Harry yips. "In late October, I get a phone call from a storage facility in Basra. Djermajian died and left a locked storage shed. Double-and-triple locked. The only documentation they had was a recent, undated shipping contract with us. They offered me the contents of the locker for the two months arrears on the shed. I remembered him saying he wasn't worried about the cost—"

"You don't hear that too often—"

"I figured it was worth the two months arrears, surely, just to find out. I could have spent that amount on lottery tickets."

"I don't remember you going to Basra."

"Absolutely not; it's dangerous and bad coffee since the Americans came. I needed someone we could trust—someone who would recognize obscure and valuable objects and who wasn't too far away, because I didn't have major plane fare. So I called Stacia."

"Who's Stacia?" I'm not surprised by the look on Sara's face but even Amina, who seemed to be snoozing, is now wide-eyed curious.

-So who is Stacia?

Stacia Olyvegnaya was the worst office romance I ever had. Absolutely bewitching woman and brilliant. Exquisite taste, worked for us for five years so she knew the whole menagerie—cars, watches, bags, jewelry, fine art.

-Ships passing in the night, as they say?

Do they say that here?

-I read it somewhere.

Worse than that. We both wanted *more*. Funny thing about *more*—you can never actually have it. She eventually went home to Georgia.

-Not Atlanta, I'm guessing.

Tblisi.

So Harry continues: "Stacia flies down, opens the shed, finds a machine shop and one crate. After uncrating, she emails me, instructing me to download several programs onto my computer. A messaging program where everything's in code—

"Encrypted—"

"That's it—and a few other things so I wasn't going through the regular Internet. I had to pay Clarice's nephew to do it but we got them running. Then she sent me photographs of the device Djermajian had left behind. Stupid looking thing, crude but a working nuclear device, built to be transported and set off remotely."

"Where the fuck did Djermajian get that?"

"Apparently, he *built* it. Stacia dropped some petty cash in Karachi and found out that Djermajian used to work at Dr. Khan's skunk works, making nuclear weapons for the Pakistanis and selling them out the back door to anyone with money and bad intentions. He was Khan's quality-control man and a bit of a hoarder. Whenever ten of something came in, he'd reject one as sub-standard and keep it for himself. Over several years, he put together the pieces he needed."

"How did he get the plutonium?" Sara asks.

"Who knows? Former Soviet states, Saadam's nuclear program—"

"Sadaam's WMD's were a fabrication."

"He had no *active* programs in 2003—his nuclear program was shut down by Israeli bombs in the early 80's. But the sites were still intact when the US went in—they were just too busy securing oil fields to bother about plutonium. Stacia assured me that, wherever they got it, this was a working device. It was leaking radiation like an old Fiat leaks oil."

-Just a moment. How would Stacia—your office romance, schooled in fashion and cars—recognize a nuclear device in the raw?

Before moving to Paris, she graduated the Moscow Mechanical Institute 1987 as a nuclear physicist. Worked on Soviet military reactors and then with NATO, decommissioning warheads.

-You'd take her word it was a functioning device?

If she said it was, it was. Let's face it—if it wasn't, you wouldn't be here questioning me.

-Without a bomb, you would still be guilty of several serious offenses.

There's my point—if this was a simple case, I'd be in a Wadiiran jail wondering what limbs I was going to lose instead of here, talking to you. There's something delicate here that needs covering up, which means it's a real bomb.

-And, where is this Stacia now?

Somewhere secure in the Ural Mountains. But if we're in trouble, she'll come out of the woodwork.

-Is that a threat?

I'm not threatening. I'm separating the meaningful details from the loose ends, in case you're thinking about trying to bury this thing. It won't bury, take my word for it.

-We'll see. However, if it is buried in your favor—can we count on Stacia remaining secure?

Stacia will say whatever Harry asks her to say.

-Harry...

Yes, Harry's part of the price. Harry, Diamante, Sara and I all walk away together, that's the package.

-What if that isn't possible? What if, as the gangster movies say, there has to be a fall guy?

Let's get to the end and check the cards then.

So Harry stalks the wall of windows, all worked up, gesticulating wildly and flexing his baritone. "Who knows what happened? Maybe Djermajian couldn't find a buyer or died before he could complete the sale. I'd taken possession by claiming the shed so I couldn't just leave it there—but where could I move it? The whole thing weighed on me for months—"

"Months? You didn't *tell* anyone?" I burst. "You didn't tell me?"

"You were out of town a lot—and I couldn't involve you, you see. You've spent a decade protecting me—figuring out the rules, the guidelines, how to do the dance without getting caught. This time, I wanted to protect *you*.

"And then, there was the carbomb in London and the club shooting in the Fifth Arrondissement and the carbomb in Belgium and then the Rue Breguet and I started thinking, maybe there *was* a point to it. I just had to move the bomb. You remember Mr. Lazlo—"

"Lazlo! Jesus!" Explain to Sara: "Serbian, regional arms dealer. Scumbag."

"Well, he was available," Harry apologizes. "I wrote a certificate for the *Mercury Venture*, contacted Mr. Lazlo to pick up the device and deliver it, delicate handling, to the ship."

"You didn't tell that snake what he was moving—"

"I'm forgetful, not stupid. Stacia left it securely crated before she went home."

"So you shipped it and came out here to receive it. And you hired Rene and Proto to keep me busy until you were done—?"

Harry nods, taking credit eagerly.

"But then why set the *police* after Nicky?" Sara asks.

"What are you talking about?"

"The false charge—that I smuggled the Rue Breguet bomb into Paris."

Harry's eyes open wide. "I didn't do *that*. I wouldn't— no, never."

"You're sure?" I demand. "You haven't forgotten, you didn't by mistake?"

"No, no, I swear. It's all worked out brilliantly—other than you two showing up here."

"Right, okay—a brilliant plan to ship a nuclear weapon here to blow up a pumping station."

And here Harry's face deepens, an expression I've seen only a very few times.

"I'm not blowing up the pumping station, my boy. I'm blowing up the Arabian Peninsula. I'm blowing up the modern world."

He rushes to retrieve a whiteboard from behind the drapes, tilting it to give us a good look at a map tacked in place, surrounded by scribbles and notes around the edges.

"Here's Ras Tanura and here—" he traces a spidery line across the entire Arabian Peninsula, highlighting oil fields along the way "— is the pipeline. The ship sails to the mouth of the pipeline and the bomb explodes. Yes, it takes out the pumping station—but what matters is, nuclear fire flies the length of the pipeline, lighting the oil in underground oilfields throughout the peninsula. Whoosh! In a day, thirty or forty per cent of the world's oil is destroyed or rendered so radioactive, no one can touch it for a century. What's left becomes so expensive, it's useless."

He pauses, taking us in, jubilant. We all stare at each other, stone silent.

"Would that *work*?" I ask weakly.

"Maybe," Yusuf says. Sara nods.

"Tomorrow morning, there's a convention of sun worshippers right below us!" Harry gestures out the window, at a coastline amphitheater facing north—facing Ras Tanura. "12,000 people, having traveled from all over the world to celebrate the annular solar eclipse, just as the bomb goes off. Twelve thousand cellphone cameras! I didn't plan it but there it is! Greatest show on Earth!"

He faces us again, eyes wide, mouth agape with desire.

"Do you know what happens? The bomb is so hot, it turns the sand—all that sand—to glass. We'll literally be blinded by the light, during an eclipse. It's *biblical*."

"You'll kill millions of people!" Sara says.

"Oh no, I won't," Harry grabs back his laptop to answer. "Look! There's a website for it!" The legend atop the page reads NUKEMAP; the screen shows a bullseye over

Ras Tanura. "You see? Here's a 36-kiloton device like mine! They estimate the direct injuries from the blast at 8,600, tops! Most of the fallout drifts over the Gulf and dissipates! Even with fallout deaths over time, we're talking only 578,000 dead and 964,000 injured—even with the injured, it's under a million!"

The room has gone silent, the audience exhausted and defeated by the evening's speaker. The sound of his words echoing off the walls is lunacy. Yet Harry's thrilled. It's charming, brilliant, as far as he's concerned, because, at this juncture, any train of thought he can bring to conclusion seems brilliant to him.

"They're people." It's Amina speaking now, quiet but coiled. "That's our entire population."

"They hate you," Harry says, brutal. Amina recoils. The family is not used to being spoken to like this. It's a dangerous moment.

"But Harry…why?"

"*Why?*" Harry's voice rises an octave. "Because it *has* to be done! Look at the Rue Breguet! And three more times in Paris in as many years! And Mumbai and Madrid—and the World Trade Center! Look at the damage there—and all the damage in retaliation. They kill three thousand in New York, maybe a thousand in Europe and we kill—who knows? Half a million? A million civilians in Iraq, Afghanistan, Syria, Yemen? Which makes them want to kill us even more! It has to stop. All I'm doing is saving us from ourselves!"

We're wheezing. We're wiping our noses, our upper lips, our foreheads. I can't remember a room so electric with so little going on.

"This area's no different, really, from Ireland, Kosovo, Central Africa, India and Pakistan, Nepal and China, you name it. They're all squabbling with each other, hating each other, sniping and killing each other. Except we don't have millions of troops tied up in any of those other places. Why? We all know why. Because of *the OIL!*

"We're addicted. We always need *more.* We know we should quit, the signs of self-destruction surround us and the means to quit are available. But, like any junkie, our need for *more* distorts and corrupts everything else. Fatah and Hamas, Shiite and Sunni, Arabs and Persians, these are *worldwide* issues now instead of local petty arguments— simply because this place has what we crave."

"The West own the oil companies," Sara says.

"True—we're so efficient, the addict *and* the pusher—these poor slobs just happen to live where the garden grows. But what shall we do—wait for the addicts to seek treatment? No—we have to go cold turkey. And we will, tomorrow morning."

Another long silence.

"But again, why *us*, Harry?" Diamante asks. "We're not the people who change history."

"Right," I add. "We're the ones who watch from a distance and pick up what falls on the floor, or what we can get to fall on the floor. Since when do we stoop to changing the world?"

The look in his eyes is naked, infinitely sad—and defeated. I've never seen *this* face before, not ever.

"I'm sliding off into the blue, Nicky. Nothing to lose anymore."

"You're just tired," Diamante coos. "A few days—"

"I *am* tired, my darling, but a few days? If only! When I had the vision, when I saw it all in front of me, it felt like destiny, don't you see? It didn't take me ten minutes with a map to recognize the rightness of the thing."

"They'll put you in jail for the rest of your life," Sara says, anguished.

"I won't spend a day in a proper jail," Harry settles back in his chair, imperious. "A competent solicitor and a well-spoken physician and the worst I'll end up is a locked ward with rubber walls."

"It won't work," Yusuf addresses us now, with a shocking competence—here's the Cambridge-educated prince behind the gangsta pose. "You think we haven't planned for this? As soon as oil goes to five dollars a gallon, solar and wind become economical. We've already laid out the world's largest solar farm—we've got the sun and we've bought the acreage. The transmission lines to Europe will take less than three years in an emergency. You destroy the oil, we'll keep our power, thank you."

And finally, that is that. No one has anything to say. It's the aftermath of a fifteen-round fight, the survivors in their corners, semi-conscious on their stools.

Harry pulls a bottle of champagne off the upright cart and pulls the foil off the top. "Let's drink to Oblivion," he says. "Going blind for the cause."

Yusuf's deference is gone. "Give me my phone—I'm calling Rahim."

"You're not calling anyone!" Harry says firmly.

"Phone or not, I'm leaving," Yusuf glares at Diamante. "You're not shooting me."

"I STILL HAVE THE REMOTE!!" Harry thunders, pulling a plastic lozenge from his pocket and wagging it over his head.

A moment later, Diamante and I have jumped him and I hold the gizmo in my hand.

"You have *a remote control*?" I scream. "They gave you a *remote control for a nuclear bomb*?" And I do something reckless, because I know, deep down, it isn't. I push the top left button at the same time as the 'On' switch. The television across the room immediately lights up. I switch it off.

"What were you told this would do?"

"I can arm the bomb from here," Harry says but the confidence is oozing out of him.

"This thing wouldn't arm a set of Lego's."

His face collapses. Not just wrong, but humiliated, a fool. Here is the fear Harry has always run from—disguising himself, shuffling *personae* like suits, conjuring legends and schemes and finally commandeering a nuclear device to upend civilization—the lifelong fear of being exposed as a fraud, of proving his snooty clients right when they snickered their way out of our office. God, do I *hate* this moment.

Diamante's pistol is still pointed at Yusuf's forehead. I should tell him to back off—he certainly isn't going to shoot—but I can't.

"You can't leave, Yusuf, not yet," I say. "Not till we get sorted out."

"What if there really is a bomb?" Yusuf demands. "What if they didn't just take his money and run away, laughing?"

"There *is* a bomb!" Harry insists.

"If Stacia says it's a bomb, it's a bomb," I say.

"How long do you suggest we wait?" Yusuf asks and it's a fair question.

"We're not going to wait. We can't." I turn to Harry. "When does the ship dock?"

"In the morning, as the sun rises, like 6 am," he says.

"So we have several hours to play with."

"Play with? What if it gets jostled and goes off?" Yusuf asks.

"A nuclear weapon won't go off from jostling," I say.

"A *properly designed* one won't," Sara warns. "This was home-made in a shed."

"What's if it's behind schedule? Or ahead?" Yusuf continues. They're all legitimate questions.

"We can find out where they are!" Diamante starts clicking at Harry's laptop. "We've got the tracker on the container."

He logs himself into our office system and clicks through several menus. "Oh!" he says sharply. I remember being on a small plane once and hearing the pilot say "Oh!" in just that tone. You *really* don't want pilots or surgeons or people tracking your stray nuclear device saying, "Oh!" in quite that voice.

Yusuf, Sara and I converge over Diamante's shoulder, peering at the screen. "Where is it?"

"It's right out *there*," he points over Amina's head, out the windows to the Gulf. "But it's not heading the right direction."

On the app, the ship looks so close—it's probably visible out the window, if we only knew which ship it was. But it's sailing at a steady clip in the other direction, toward the far coast of the Gulf.

"Where's it going?" Harry asks.

Yusuf and Sara answer simultaneously. "Iran."

Diamante looks at me and I know what's coming. When he says "We've got to stop that ship," like it's something we do every other weekend, I bury my head in my hands.

NEGOTIATION

-At that point, going directly to Prince Rahim wouldn't have been a better decision?

Yusuf suggested that exact thing, of course.

"I can't let you," I tell him.

"Are you insane?"

"This is the real world. Think politics," I say. "If Rahim sends out commandos or fighter planes and takes the ship, it's at very least a diplomatic incident. Based on what? Our word? If it goes to Iran, on the other hand, it's gone, it's not Rahim's problem. Why take action when the problem's sailing away all by itself at the moment? He's not going to do anything—and in his position, that's the right answer."

"That's not your decision," Yusuf says.

"Oh yes, it is," Sara says. "Prince Rahim's life is politics. He's better off letting this go—but we *can't*, you see? We're stuck in the real world. We created this problem, it's our responsibility." She stares at me and I nod. Yes, that's the answer. I don't know what to do about it but I know she's right.

Yusuf goes quiet for a long moment and then his face changes. "So what's the plan, dog?"

"We've got a big check from your brother. That'll make a suitcase stuffed with cash, more than the captain of a Gulf freighter's ever seen, I'll bet." I turn to Diamante. "We've got to have a contact number for the ship, right?" He starts clicking to find it.

"You can't call them as you," Sara says.

"Huh? Why not?"

"Think about it—they *have* to be the ones who set the police on you. They're the only player left. Whoever's on that ship, they saw your signature on the cert and wanted to make sure you wouldn't interfere with them."

"That's got to be right," I realize. "Harry, you should talk to them. Harry?"

Harry is silent, withdrawn into the deep cushions of his chair. He dismisses me with a wave—a passive, helpless surrender. He's not lost anymore—lost would be better than this. He's totally in the here and now, totally aware of what's happening, aware for the first time of what he's done.

"Get us on the ship," Yusuf changes gears. "We'll clean the place up."

"Who's 'we'?"

"No!" Amani howls. "Absolutely positively 'no', brother!"

"My boys. We did six weeks of tactical training with Special Forces last summer. We packin', dog! I got a Tec-9, Hassan's got a Uzi!" He sees the look on my face. "Hey, fuck the Israelis; they make *great* fucking guns! You should see us at the range!"

"Categorically 'no'."

"A ship at sea isn't—"

"They're fucking sailors, dog—we can take 'em!"

"Tell him 'no'," Amina begs. "Just tell him."

This trip keeps uncovering new horizons for bad ideas. I might pay to watch Yusuf and buddies doing

'Firefight at Sea' on pay-per-view, but I sure as hell am not putting our future in their hands.

"No fighting," I say. "We'll outpay them instead."

"I thought I already did," Harry says, stalking the windows and my first thought is to make sure he can't get onto the balcony. If we don't fix this, Harry's a goner.

"You did until they found out what was on board," Sara says.

"You think they know?"

"They *must*. Otherwise, why set the police on Nicky? And now, they're delivering the bomb to Iran." She turns to me. "You really think we can outbid a government?"

"No deal's a good one if you don't survive it. Give me your phone." She does and I dial the number on the cert.

Miraculously, it picks up. No greeting but the line is open.

"My name is Millard Hastings," I say. "I have a shipment on board that I want to re-route. Can you help me with that?"

"We don't go no place but—" the voice cuts off suddenly and I hear other voices in the background. I hear

'Hastings' several times and then the voice returns. "You wanna make change, it costs money."

"Fine."

"Lotta money."

"I've got a lot of money."

"I mean a lot a lot."

"Yes, no problem."

"How I get it?"

"I want to check the shipment, make sure everything is the way I set it up."

A pause. Chatter in the back. "You come to the ship now?"

"Yes."

Where you coming from?"

"Qumrahdi."

He gives me coordinates and says they'll wait two hours. "Bring money and we see." Then he hangs up.

Diamante stares at the app on the laptop screen. "They're turning around. But once they get the money—?"

Suddenly, it's Harry who's talking. "This wasn't just money—they weren't interested until they heard Millard

Hastings." He gives me the gnarly eye. "Why are you Hastings?"

"He owns that warehouse complex in Basra. I'll bet he's got three or four containers on the ship. At least, he's a name they know. They know he has money."

"So what do we do?" Sara asks.

"What do they want? Those are HARRY'S RULES. Hopefully, they're just sailors who found the bomb and want to sell it to the highest bidder. We get there first with cash in a suitcase and convince them to sell it to us. If they weren't open to the idea, they wouldn't be turning around, would they?"

"What if it goes bad?" Yusuf asks. "You can't just leave this to chance."

"That's correct," Sara says. "We can't leave anything to chance. That's why we're locking you in the back room."

"You can't—"

Diamante's checking with me—Sara looks a lot more certain about this than I am. I nod and Diamante motions with the pistol for Yusuf to lead the way.

"I won't go! Mahmood, stop them!"

Cousin Mahmood could be a real issue, if he decides to resist. Instead, he strikes an odd pause, a moment of total helplessness, before throwing a glance at...Princess Amina, who shakes her head.

"Sorry, brother," Amina says. "I'll let you out once it's over."

"What? You can't do this!" Yusuf yells.

"You see," Sara says, "all you boys ever want to do is fight, like that's ever solved a problem in the history of the world. Amina and I have discussed it and we've had enough." She stares her laser vision right at me. "We're going to solve this without fighting."

Cousin Mahmood and Diamante stash Yusuf in the backroom, oversee Flunky changing the room's lock code using an app on his phone, check to see that the door is truly locked, then Diamante takes the phone and key card from Flunky.

"Give him the phone back," I say, "just long enough to call the desk and turn off the phone in that room."

"I'm a Prince of the Royal Family of Wadiirah!" Yusuf yells from behind the door. "You'll pay for this!"

"Yes, but we'll pay *later*," Sara says.

I wander over to Princess Amina, who's taken a seat outside Yusuf's door. "And when this is all over," I tell her, "I'll do my best to make it right with your Uncle Khalil."

Her face goes cold. "I don't think you will," she says. "Families depended on him. When he failed them, when he was disgraced, he cut off his own hand. It was appropriate, but I don't think you can make that right."

And there you feel the air go out of the room. There's no drama in the sound of her voice—the story may be history to her, maybe crazy ancient family history—but she knows what she's saying. The taste is bitter going down. Across the room, I see Harry's face collapse. We've gone a lot of years without being confronted with the consequences of our actions. But now, here they are and, in a way, all the more awful for being so deadpan.

~~~~

An hour later, we're on a seaplane, circling the *Mercury Venture* and bracing for landing.

-Who's in the party now?

Harry, Sara, Diamante and me.

-Unarmed?

Unarmed. I'm not giving them reason to kill us. My conviction is that most people don't kill without reason.

-You're an optimist.

At least I tried it once.

As we climb the ladder to the heaving deck, a group of sailors watch us from above, clutching their guns uncomfortably. That discomfort would be more reassuring if they looked like they'd eaten well recently. It's hard to reason with a hungry man. They frisk us as we come onboard. Sara knees the first one who tries it and the next is logarithmically more respectful.

The captain is a bit smaller than most of his sailors; long wisps of greasy dark hair sprout from beneath an oversized once-was-white sailor's cap out of an old movie. He watches quietly from the bridge until we've all been given the once-over. I try to catch his eye, just to signal good faith but he won't make contact.

And then, the door at the base of the bridge opens and we're surrounded by soldiers in black. These boys look *plenty* comfortable with their automatic weapons. I recognize the uniforms—Iranian Revolutionary Guard, black-on-black, kidnapper's ski mask, only the eyes and mouth exposed. The darkest of the dark, the truest of true believers, forming a very proper tactical formation around us in seconds. Just the way they step into position would quell most revolutions.

Once they're in place, from the doorway comes Bossman. Nobody has to tell us he's the Bossman—the stillness, the focus, those bright, creative, cruel eyes say it all.

"Who's Hastings?" he says in just the commanding voice I expect.

Decision Time: Is this somebody I play with or somebody I level with? Big stakes if I guess wrong.

"Well, nobody actually," I say, wincing, but this doesn't faze him at all.

"You're acting for Hastings?" he says.

"We all are," Sara says quickly.

For the first time, he pauses to take us all in. We bring a smile to his face, but not a friendly one. "So, you're—a democracy?" he asks. Clearly, this is a laugh line.

"We're a team," I say.

"Congratulations," he answers, the smile now chilling. "You all come down into the hold with me—now!"

I've never been on a real freighter, a real working ship, before and this one is clearly ancient. The smell of motor oil, curry and piss, the groaning of the hull and clatter of the mains, the damp corridors, jury-rigged wiring hanging just below the ceiling, all seem relics of an era long past. I expect Humphrey Bogart and Sydney Greenstreet bantering below deck. Normally, that would be Harry and me, but at the moment, Harry's neutered, empty—silent, head down, tail between his legs. I could know how he feels—but, right now, I can't let myself.

Three levels down and over to the cargo bay. Bossman throws open the hatch and leads us in. The place is brightly-lit, which in itself seems odd—cargo bays are made to be dark and dingy, someone's gone to the trouble of bringing in lights. These guys have been on this ship a while.

As we circle round the first row of containers, I realize the terrible mistake I've made.

"Okay, Millard Hastings' team—explain *this* to me!" Bossman demands.

Planking from ten or more custom containers litter the floor. No routine enclosures, these—rubber-padded, beautifully-fitted-and-built, as they should be.

Under the lights, stripped of their enclosures, stands Millard Hastings' cargo for this trip: Handcut limestone columns five stories high. The pediment that sat atop them a thousand years before Christ, elaborate scenes of gods and men and mythical creatures, stories instantly familiar though I can't remember ever reading one of them. Dazzling shimmering mosaics, cyclopses and humans and distant galaxies, in colors I've never seen before. Astounding creatures—winged bulls with men's faces, hawk faces with women's bodies— towering just below the thirty-foot ceiling. And more.

"You know what this is?" Bossman demands.

"You tell us," Sara answers, but her voice is hushed, reverential. This display would inspire awe and humility in anyone who ever read a history book or looked twice at a piece of art.

"These are the prototypes for the modern world," Bossman says and is it possible to argue? "Tile from the greatest churches of antiquity. Sentries from the gates of heaven, maybe the same ones seen by Abraham in Ur. A statue of Alexander the Great, carved by a man who probably saw him alive. The sacred treasures of our culture. Not Iran's culture, *all* our culture, the shared culture of the Middle East, of the Judeo-Christian-Islamic world."

"Aleppo," I murmur.

-That wasn't smart thinking, saying it out loud.

If I'd been thinking, I never would have. It's just reaction. Not that it matters, really—Bossman is livid already. It's only clear now how tightly he's been holding himself under control.

"Maybe Aleppo, maybe Palmyra. Maybe a hundred other places. Does it matter?" His voice degrades quickly— the sound now is like metal scraping metal. "Syria's destroyed anyway, who's to say what was stolen and what destroyed? So why not loot the place for display in the homes of wealthy Americans?"

Explaining they were looted for the homes of wealthy Russian oligarchs feels like nitpicking. If it wasn't Woczynski, someone in the West or Japan surely would have made the same deal.

"So?" Bossman homes in on me, challenging. "You have *nothing* to say? No defense? No excuses, no others to blame?" Sure I have—Millard Hastings is to blame, if only I hadn't already decided to *be* him.

It all makes sense, in the ghastly way life makes sense sometimes. Millard Hastings owns the warehouse complex where the bomb was. The *Mercury Venture* makes its pick-up from the complex—our one container and his who-knows-how-many. Our bomb and his *History of the World as We Know It.*

We're at a dead stop. Any plan I might have had is completely out of gas. And so am I.

And then I hear Harry pipe up. He's alive! And fighting, bless him, or at least trying to figure out how.

"I'm not with Hastings," he says, a bit hesitantly. "That was a story I made up to get on board."

Whatever end-around he's got in mind, this doesn't have a good effect. Bossman's paranoia level definitely seems to kick up a notch.

"Explain yourself—*details!*" he demands and Harry goes silent again, chastened. He's reached for the kind of absurd outburst that has so often pulled us out of the fire at the crucial moment. But he conjures no magic this day. His heart isn't in it.

That's when we hear rotors mashing and shouts from on-deck.

STEALING A SHIP

We crowd into the landing outside the cargo bay, herded by Bossman and his troops.

"Three parties!" he calls and clearly, this is a well-rehearsed drill. Two groups of soldiers rush off to the fore and aft staircases. We wait with Bossman and four others, counting off half a minute, and then begin the rapid sprint up the central staircase, to the deck of the ship.

At the doorway there, two of his soldiers await, reporting in a burst. Bossman zooms in on me, not necessarily angry but very determined.

"Your friends are outside. Westerners with serious weapons."

Huh? I'm totally thrown. Amina and Cousin Mahmood are keeping Yusuf from calling Rahim—who else would send Westerners with serious weapons?

"They are deceived," Bossman continues. "They have merely taken the ship's crew. My men heard their helicopters coming and disappeared off the deck." He listens to chatter on a previously-invisible earpiece and then says, "Go!" Is he speaking Persian or English? I'm totally lost but it's not hard to figure out what he's saying.

His men burst from the hatches, pouring out of the fore and aft stairs, and swiftly complete the same ring they made around us when we came aboard. There's shouting and a quick scuffle but then it all goes quiet and tense.

Sara turns to me with her most serious face and says, "No fighting. You promised—"

"All we've got here is people who live to fight." I glance at Harry for support here—she's asking the impossible. But he's still lost among his own regrets.

"Your specialty," she persists, "is getting other people to decide that what they want is what you want them to want." The way she says it, it sounds so *complicated*.

"You said that was stupid. And morally wrong."

"Well, here's your chance to convince me," she answers and basically it's Sara's mic drop. *Here's your plan, buddy—make it stick.*

In the middle of the deck stand six soldiers in American desert camo and face paint—?

"Lay down your arms and surrender peacefully—we outnumber you," Bossman says.

"You've got numbers but I've got the crew!" yells the American leader in a ridiculous Texas accent and I find myself hurtling out the door.

"*Dieter*? What the fuck—"

"Get out of the line of fire!"

"No fire! No shooting, anybody!" I yell, stationing myself between the lines of soldiers and appealing to Bossman. "You can't have a firefight here."

"We can be in Iranian waters within ten minutes," he replies. "My crew holds the bridge." Clearly, he's aiming this at Dieter. "We will easily win any firefight—"

"That's not my point—you can't fight here because of what's in the hold."

"Is *this* Hastings?" he says, pointing at Dieter. "Is he responsible—?"

"No—not that—I'm worried about the *other* shipment in the hold!"

"Shipping Certificate 942 762 837," Diamante recites, over my shoulder. "Construction equipment for Ras Tanura," and judging by Bossman's expression, *this* definitely rings a bell.

"The certificate you doctored to get me thrown in jail in Paris," I say and now the bells are chiming a chorus.

"What are you doing with *them*?" Dieter demands in his usual sledgehammer tone. "Where's my fucking Porsche?"

"I'm not with—you're here for the *car*?"

"You bought it with my money! You used my company ID to transport it! Where is it?"

Bossman, sensibly, ignores Dieter. "A firefight won't set off a bomb."

"Not *if it's designed correctly*," I say again and I can see he understands my concern.

"What are you talking about? Where's my fucking 917?"

"Who is this idiot and what does he want?"

My fingers pause, tingling, at the rim of Pandora's Box but, as happens so often lately, no answer occurs to me but the truth. Maybe I'm really too old for this kind of work. "That's—it's *his* shipment below."

"So *he* is Hastings?" Bossman says.

"He's Hastings' man."

"I thought *you* were Hastings' man."

"Why are you talking to *him*?" Dieter yells. "I'm one second from blowing this whole place to Kingdom come."

"Just let us get this straightened out," I yell. "*Then* you two can kill each other!" They both look at me like I'm deranged but that's not *my* fault.

"I—used Hastings' name to get on board," I explain to Bossman. "But I'm here for...the *other* package." Bossman's eyes widen. "I was hoping we could buy it back but once I met you, I knew that wasn't going to work."

"Three-two—?" Dieter ticks off the time. His boys level their guns and the Iranians do the same, facing each other at close range.

I step up to the line again, determined, arms up in both directions. "Nobody shoots! Dieter, have your men put down their guns and the Iranians will do the same!"

"We will not!"

"Are you fucking nuts?"

"Just long enough for all of us to go down into the hold," I yell at Bossman. "Just long enough so everyone understands what's going on down there. Once you both know what's at stake, you're going to want to talk, not shoot."

"That's stupid!" Dieter says. "I *always* want to shoot! We're *soldiers!*" And what I hear in my head when he says that is '*warriors*'—I find myself mouthing the word and see Sara catch me at it. And see that she remembers, that it has the same significance for her that it has for me.

"Dieter, we've been talking about the shipment this boat picked up *in Basra, just the other day, at Hastings' warehouse.*" I'm speaking slowly and enunciating, the way I would to a child, and dawn slowly breaks in that foggy mind of his. "A shipment these boys have already opened."

"Sssssshit," Dieter hisses, with the same involuntary impulse that made me say 'Aleppo' out loud.

"By the way, Dieter?" I wait till he refocuses on me. "That isn't the punchline, either. Not even close. Have one of your men lay down his weapons and one of the Iranians will do the same." I turn to Bossman and he reluctantly agrees.

Dieter nods to one of his soldiers, who ejects the clip, puts down his rifle and unbuckles his pistol and ammo belt. Dieter nods more vehemently and the same soldier pulls open a patch in his vest and removes another pistol from a hidden holster there, then another small one from a compartment on his hip, a long knife from his thigh and several ammo clips from across his back. I realize this is going to take a while.

The first Iranian soldier follows suit and, for half an hour, we dance the laborious synchronized swim of the psychotically paranoid.

In the meantime, I'm furiously toting the odds and weighing the angles and the sums keep coming out bad, each and every way I can think of.

I'm in over my head. For years, I've managed to rig the game in my favor—by now, I've taken that tilt for granted. But what comes clear to me in the moment is that I've always had a built-in advantage—I was always playing my own game. I chose the players and the stakes and the terms. I made up HARRY'S RULES to keep things in bounds. I dressed the marionettes, pulled the strings and never walked into a room without knowing first three ways out and their precise locations.

The problem now is, this *isn't* my game.

And as I watch Dieter and Bossman at work, I get the sinking realization it isn't *their* game either. They're into Round Three of a staring contest, snarling at each other and openly resentful of my intervention, so desperate to be in control, they clearly would prefer to kill us all (and die themselves) than be forced to cooperate. Fighting is their role, it's all they know and all my alternatives, all my attempts to widen their horizons, only make them feel more imperiled.

Because a roleplayer is only safe within the set confines of his role and, I realize now, every single person we've met is just a roleplayer in this game. We haven't met a soul who can *grant* protection, only accept it. Even Rahim was so concerned to know who was protecting *me*. Dieter made Hastings nervous, the same way I'm throwing Dieter off his game of conquer or die, the only alternatives he's able to consider. We're all of us just dangling by the strings.

It's time to cut the cord.

I need an outside force, someone who doesn't even notice the stupid bloody game, who's aware of the real danger here, someone who hopefully sees more in life than just a win column.

The Iranians have us all boxed with the ship's crew into a tight little group. Harry towers over the captain; I can barely see the man's face because of that stupid oversized hat of his. I elbow him and whisper, "Do you have a plan to take back the ship?" and if a man could actually die laughing, I fear that's what I've done to him. He'll die happy, if nothing else, considering the guffawing and hacking and he and Harry elbowing each other, thanks a lot, pal. "You really think any of them are going to leave us alive once they get what they want?"

Harry goes ashen-faced and the captain finally stops laughing. "I know," he murmurs. "But we're not fighters. Not against *them*."

My heart sinks. I understand, how could I not? These aren't men, they're not even warriors—they're creatures, with their muscles and their arsenal and their steroidal antsy aggression. He's listening but nowhere near self-nominating yet.

RULE ONE: KNOW YOUR PARTNER. *Think*, Nicky! Who's in front of you?

Asian, mid-fifties, not physically powerful, in a world where physical intimidation is common. He won't have had a lot of schooling but, in his world, a ship's captain is still a powerful, responsible position. His crew may be underfed and overworked and some of them might have been taken on board against their will but they follow his orders and work as his team. He's learned navigation, charts, radio, several languages (good English) and people management. In his world, he's a formidable guy.

And, at the moment, he's deciding the fate of himself and his crew. He knows about the bomb in the hold and he can see the weaponry being laid out on deck before him. These are the biggest stakes he's ever faced. He can't get this wrong and there's a hundred ways to go wrong here.

RULE THREE: TELL THEM WHAT THEY WANT TO HEAR.

What does he *need* to hear?

"Of course, you're right. They're the fighters, it's all they know. So what if you let them fight? You're the *captain*," I improvise, trying to keep my voice from shaking.

"You know this ship better than any man alive. You know the weak seams, the leaking compartments, which ladders are hanging by a thread and which corridors go nowhere. Lure them, a few at a time, down below. Make noise and slip away. Draw them down blind hallways and into places you can trap them. Lead them a merry chase. Confuse them. Use what you know to beat them. Save us all."

His mouth sets, his eyes go dark. What's wrong with the pitch?

"Why do white people lie all the time?" he asks. Just like that. No guile, no games, just letting it hang out. *Tell me I'm wrong*, he dares, *then I'll* know *you're a liar!* I can only imagine the litany of crap this poor man's dealt with over the decades. "We not *people* to you," he continues and what do I say to that? I stand dumbfounded.

Sara leans in. "They *do* lie, you're right," she nods. "They lie to us, too, all the time." I don't think the captain's much of a feminist—I doubt the issue comes up a lot on board—but this is Sara's moment, she's got his attention. "You're not in their club and neither are we. But what I've learned about men, over the years, is that the ones you trust are the ones who ask for help, who admit they need it."

You and your crew," I say, as simple as I can say anything, "are the only ones who can make this happen."

Now he looks me squarely in the eye. "And what do we need *you* for?" he says. "They don't want us. Maybe they let us go."

"*Maybe*," I question.

"I know," he nods. "Maybe not. But maybe."

He's got a right, I guess. This is a challenge but, as I'd be reminding Harry, it's also a buying signal. I need to *close* him, *now*.

"Show him the case," I tell Diamante.

He pulls off his backpack, opens it, shows the captain the stacks inside and gives him a couple stacks to examine, which he stuffs inside his jacket.

"Okay," he repeats. "So what do we need *you* for?" Now that he knows where the money is...

"That's a nuclear weapon in the hold. If somebody hasn't read the radiation signature yet, they will before the sun comes up. Even if you take back the ship, you're going to need somebody to look the other way—" I turn to Diamante. "You have a picture of our prisoner?"

Diamante pulls out his phone and displays his photo of grumpy Prince Yusuf of the Royal face and Cousin Mahmood, standing next to Sara and Harry.

"We have friends," I say. "We can work our way out of this—if we make it to shore alive."

"Give me suitcase."

"When we take the ship back."

The Captain starts conferring with his First Mate.

The disarming finally concludes, leaving two members of each camp guarding the arms stash. Dieter, Bossman, Harry and I descend to the hold.

Dieter's not totally obtuse—as soon as he sees the lights, he knows there's a problem. When he rounds the first turn and catches sight of Hastings' Syrian treasure, he shrinks a couple of inches involuntarily. "Whoa!" is all that comes out but, from a block of granite like him, that's a soliloquy.

"Any excuses?" Bossman demands. "Any explanations for stealing our history?"

"What did you tell him?" Dieter wheels on me.

"He knew before we got here."

Dieter sighs and takes in the winged bulls, the mosaics and the face of Alexander—and here's proof that even someone with zero aesthetic sense can't help but be moved by the power of it. "Yeah, I don't want to shoot this up."

"Dieter, I told you—this *isn't* the punch line," and I wag a finger for him to follow.

Around to the next row, another uncrated container, a silver box like an old-fashioned refrigerator, lying on its side, Plexiglas windows baring banks of switches and diodes and blooming LED's. Dieter is mute, unable or unwilling to engage, looking over the instruments repeatedly, trying to get the sums to come out differently. "What the fuck is it?" he says.

"Either it's a sixty-five-megaton device or I've seriously overpaid," Harry shrugs. Suddenly, he's nonchalant, reassured, confident. It's as though he's forgotten everything that's gone wrong and we're all just bantering in the office. "It's my plan and my bomb."

"The plan may be yours," says Bossman, "but the bomb is ours."

"Excuse me?" He's talking! What happened!

Before Bossman can answer, we hear shuffling near the doorway. Two soldiers—one Iranian and one American contractor—peek through the door, ostensibly checking on the safety of their leaders.

"Maybe we should take this to the bridge?" I suggest. "Where there's a closed door? Assuming you feel comfortable closing a door on them."

"I know my men," Bossman says and Dieter shouts, "Me too."

"Good for you," I say. "Which of you ordered them down here?"

"They use their discretion," Dieter says as we near the doorway, but clearly he's uncomfortable with the pair standing there.

"Right," says Bossman, with the same body language. They make sure the hold is locked before we all head up on deck.

Just before arriving, we squeeze past the First Mate and cook, supporting a vomiting sailor down the steps, this group escorted by two soldiers—one Iranian and one American contractor, each carrying handguns.

"Does it worry you that your guys are working together without you?" I ask. Dieter and Bossman both answer 'No' immediately but they don't look happy.

On deck, Diamante's deep in discussion with several sailors.

-So you knew what was coming?

Not a clue. It's just one more vial of nitroglycerin bouncing around in the back of the truck to me.

The sky is bleeding black to purple fog. The ship is moving slowly—we can hear the sonar ping but can't see the waves a quarter-mile ahead.

On the bridge, two Iranian soldiers man the controls. Bossman settles immediately into the captain's chair. Dieter, resentful, takes the seat at the pilot's desk opposite. Harry, Sara and I stand around the navigation table and Diamante leans against the communications rack, plugging in his phone to charge.

"Those phones will be the end of your civilization," Bossman says.

"*You* use them enough, I see," Sara says. Bossman has two on his belt and a Beats bluetooth headset in his ear.

"We *intend* to be the end of your civilization," he smiles, leaning back in his chair. "The bomb, as I say, is ours. We commissioned it several years ago, when the Obama talks stalled. The Supreme Leader approved the project as a contingency—it would have allowed us to catch up on lost time, if necessary. Of course, we made arrangements through middlemen. Then the talks picked up, we told our contact to store the device safely until we could decide the next step. He didn't reply—the next we heard, he was dead. We knew the device was somewhere in Basra but no more than that."

"Why on earth did he move it through Basra?"

"No one's checking the radiation of packets *leaving* Basra," Bossman explains. "And the only people who could move such a thing securely—without being raided or arrested—are the Americans. And most of them have no ideology. If you pay, they don't ask questions. We waited until the device finally appeared the other day and took the ship as soon as it set sail."

"And doctored the shipping certificate to set the Paris police on us—"

"We couldn't have you interfering. We had no idea why you wanted it."

"I wanted to blow up Ras Tanura with it," Harry mutters.

"You *what?*" Dieter nearly bounces out of his seat.

"I still think it's a good idea."

"It's a brilliant idea," Bossman says, fascinated.

"You can't do that!" Dieter says.

"Of course I can," Harry argues. "It actually suits you both brilliantly. We drive the price of oil up tenfold overnight, leaving Iran as the last major supplier. And we start at least a decade of war between Saudi Arabia and Iran. Since no sane politician would send American troops into another war in the Middle East, contractors like you, Dieter, would have to do the fighting." Harry smiles. "War lines so many pockets, doesn't it?"

Bossman's smile is ironic. "But it wouldn't last. The West would crash-build solar, wind and nuclear. Then we would be on our own here, just another grubby local war."

"Yeah!" Dieter realizes, severely let down.

Bossman shakes his head. "No, I have to bring the device home—and the relics!"

"The relics are ours!" Dieter growls. "You're not getting them without a fight!" The tension level is very high, suddenly.

Harry purrs, "Of course, the other option is, you could steal it together," and the air in the room shifts.

"I can't," Bossman says. "Even if I wanted to. I have to deliver it to Bandar Abbas."

"Not if it was never here," Harry says and I can see him firing on all synapses again. The man audibles better than Joe Montana. "The bomb was a false report. Djermajian sold you a bill of goods, stole your money and played you for fools."

"I cannot go home with such a result."

"You return home a hero of the Revolution for returning the cultural artifacts in the hold, wresting them from the infidels who tried to loot your heritage."

Dieter protests immediately. "That stuff is Mr. Woczynski's!"

"They are objects," Harry says. "You can find replacements. The bomb is a one-of-a-kind. I know a man in Ras Al Khaimah, in the Emirates—right across the Gulf from Bandar Abbas—who would pay very very well for our shiny box in the hold. Hundreds of millions, probably." He fixes Dieter in that over-the-glasses look of his and raises an eyebrow. "It's a good trade. You might prefer to vanish permanently with your share of the money, somewhere Mr.—whatever his name is—will never find you."

Things get very quiet—which means, everybody's thinking it over. If Harry's brain can just hold together, we have a chance.

"Is this a *plan*?" I whisper to Harry.

"Not really," he admits. "But, to Ras Al Khaimah, we're at least heading *away* from Iran."

"I can't assist in any attack in this region," Bossman counters. We've quickly shifted from 'no' to defining our terms.

"Ireland. Central Africa. The Philippines," Harry intones. "There are so many places your bomb could find a loving home."

Why does good take endless struggle while awful takes seconds? The sky is lightening, the fog beginning to burn away. You can feel a consensus brewing.

That's when we hear gunfire—several short rat-a-tat blasts from down below.

Bossman's at the rail immediately, barking orders in Persian. Dieter is right behind him. "My men go too!"

"I'm sending three, to check what's going on."

"So three of mine go with three of yours—everything's even, that's the truce. Your guys pick up guns, so do my guys."

Bossman groans and amends his orders. Both groups of soldiers grab their weapons and rush below.

"See? We work together!" says Dieter but Bossman shakes his head.

"I serve Iran," he says, as though that settles everything. "I don't know if I can do this. I would still be responsible for what happens."

"We could bring in an expert to defuse the bomb at Ras Al Khaimah," I say. "And give you the plutonium." Harry and Dieter immediately look alarmed. "But then, Dieter would insist on keeping the other loot in the hold."

"Damn straight!" Dieter says.

"I serve Iran," Bossman reminds us. "Those treasures cannot—"

"Which Iran?" Sara asks. "The Guard? The military? The elected government? The imams? *Which* imams? The ones who want to maintain Islamist purity or the ones who feel Iran needs to open itself somewhat to the West, to take its place among the nations?"

"I have my orders," says Bossman.

"Who gave them?" I ask. "Do you know for sure you'll be comfortable with what *they* do with the bomb if you take it back?"

"I didn't worry about those things when I took the mission," he says.

"You weren't responsible for the consequences then," Sara comments.

"We're drifting to port," says the Iranian at the nav station. "Four points off the line."

"Correct for it!" Bossman snaps, irritated by the interruption. His expression hardens. "I still hold the ship. Once we dock, we'll see what my superiors wish to do with you."

"Maybe we can have a show trial," Harry says, clapping his hands.

"Which of course," I add, "would complicate Iran's attempts to move past the sanctions and rejoin the world."

"Your President is blocking the door there," Bossman says with open resentment. "We negotiated in good faith. We bent over backwards." So an open Iran *is* what he wants. He's declared himself.

"Whatever the President suggests, Europe will want the opposite," Sara pounces. "Unless there's a show trial — that would surely create an international incident."

"The first country in history," pronounces Harry, "to be drowned in tweets."

"This is not my decision to make!" Bossman raises his voice—he's getting rattled.

"It is *now*," I say. "No matter what you do, any decision you make now has political repercussions. You tip the balance." In his eyes, I see uncertainty and anxiety. This is a human being. "This is how *we* got here," I tell him in as soothing a tone as I can manage. "We didn't want to be responsible for this either."

"But now," Sara says, "like it or not, it's our decision to make." That's good, shifting the decision to 'us,' but Bossman isn't ready to sign on just yet.

"I—I can't—" he stammers and then slams his hand on the desk. "Why aren't they back yet?" he barks at Dieter, like he's second-in-command.

"Who?"

"Our men! Where are they?"

Dieter heads to the rail and, shaking his head, yells, "Vince! Take Neil and two of their guys and get below! Get this *settled*!" We hear the clatter of ammo belts being picked up and buckled, of rifles loaded and soldier boots echoing down the staircase.

And, less than ten seconds later, more gunfire—and then silence. Which makes us *all* nervous.

"You know, when I was younger," I say—I think I'm talking to Bossman but it could be Sara or just myself, "I just wanted to *win*. I wanted to be a big man, have a really beautiful girl and power and money and God knows what, I don't think I really knew what, just *everything*! I was ready to settle for having everything! And now I just want to get through to the end without breaking anything."

"I still want everything," Dieter says and I'll give him credit for honesty.

"I wanted to have fun all the time," Harry says, smiling, "and, for the most part, I do."

Sara shrugs. "I wanted a pony."

"Why aren't they fighting?" Bossman bubbles over. "Or why aren't they back?" He rounds on Dieter. "Send *everyone!*"

"I only got one guy left," Dieter says. "You've got two plus the three here."

"Not the crew but send the rest down there," Bossman says. Then he grabs Sara and me. "And them too."

"Us?"

"Leave her out of this."

"When *I* was young," Bossman says, "I wanted *respect.* You are very good at—pulling at feelings, playing on my nerves, there's another word—"

"Opportunistic?" asks Harry. "Manipulative?" *Don't help me, dammit!*

"Manipulative, that's the word," Bossman nods. "You have a gift for this kind of game, but it is not useful. So I'll make another game. Go find the crew. Convince them to surrender. If you cannot, be a human shield for my men. Either way, be useful."

"If I'm dead, you won't get anybody to defuse your bomb or buy it. And you and Dieter'll end up fighting it out. It's ridiculous."

"I have my duty," Bossman says and all I see is a stupid waste of decent material. "Get going."

Down into the bowels of the ship, prodded by guns at our backs. One of the soldiers gives Sara a white sheet that she holds in front of us as we descend stairs and ladders and prowl dark corridors, prompted by creaking doors and distant footsteps. We're calling out that we want to talk, that we've come to negotiate but we get only our own echoes in response.

"You could have tried harder to save me," Sara complains.

"And if I'd convinced him? You wouldn't have had any grounds to complain about me."

"Well, that's true."

The truth is, I've never been so frightened in my life. I asked for this—I told the captain to lead them a merry chase and he's doing it—but that still leaves Sara and me between two opposing lines of guns, and I can't summon any sort of jaunty optimism for that. My hope now is that I get shot first. I don't want to know.

There's noise, just ahead, in every hallway we enter. The soldier behind me has developed this annoying habit of poking me repeatedly in the ribs with the barrel of his rifle, pushing me toward the source of the sound. But when we arrive, there's never anyone there. Once or twice we hear footsteps scuttling to the floor above; when we double-back up the steps to catch them, there's no one in sight there either.

After a few more false leads, the soldiers prod us forward, giving us a bigger lead so we can catch the brunt of any ambush.

It's goddamn spooky. The compartments are narrow and humid, the ceiling is low and clogged with the wires for every jury-rigged 'improvement' made to communications and technology in the last sixty years.

Groans and creaks abound and any one might signal danger or not, a hungry sailor pointing a gun or a rat in a corner eating crumbs. Or somebody who knows the ship way better than we do, toying with us before skinning us for dinner. That thought has to be preying on the soldiers by now. They've gotten real quiet while the rifle barrel in my ribs is getting more insistent and painful, particularly when the boy misses and pokes me in the armpit instead. His hands aren't steady, which is no comfort either.

And then, we hear sailors—talking, scrambling and scraping noises just ahead. We rush forward and stop dead at a watertight passage, doors closed and levers thrown to the locked position. On the other side of the hatch, I hear gasps and muffled blows, like punches or kicks—kicking the floor? What's going on?

And then the noise is loud right behind us, making us all jump, right back where we were before we made this turn. The soldiers hustle us around in front of them again but I know we're all thinking the same thing: How in hell did they get *behind* us without passing? And, of course, when we emerge to the central corridor again, there's no one in sight.

We keep moving but I keep hearing that poor sucker kicking the door, over and over in my head.

"I know you don't take orders," I tell Sara. "But can you let me help you?" I say. "You said trust the man asking you for help—can you trust the man who wants to help you?"

Though there's probably nothing in the world she's less likely to want, she nods tightly and I realize she's as scared as I am.

No one's rushing now. The soldiers hear the familiar noises and do their duty, check them out, but they're spooked, thrown, tentative and cautious. It's finally occurred to them that they're not the masters of this universe and both the silence and the outbursts of distant noise are very unnerving, each in their own way. Several times, I jump at a sudden sound and find that stupid gun barrel up under my arm again.

And then, we approach another watertight chamber, the hatches hanging open. And I see a hat hanging in the corridor beyond. The captain's stupid oversized white cap bobs jauntily from a pipe against the wall, just on the other side of the exit hatch.

And here again is that feeling of *knowing*, the feeling I had when I threw in with Harry, when I went for Sara, long before I knew how much she would mean to me. In the moment, again, I *know*.

I stop short, like I did earlier when startled by a sound—and there's that gun barrel, poking me under my armpit. This time, I grab the muzzle with both hands and shove it backwards with all my might. The stock strikes the soldier hard in the belly and he doubles over with a gasp.

"Go!" I yell, grabbing Sara, the two of us bolting for the exit.

"Stop!" our other soldier yells, of course. Which fills all the time necessary for us to trip over the exit door and fall through the hatch onto the really hard steel floor behind it.

And suddenly, there are sailors all over the place, emerging from side compartments and slamming shut the watertight hatches we just exited—and, from what we can hear, the hatches on the other end, the entry doors to the compartment. Leaving our soldiers locked helplessly—and loudly—inside.

"Open up! We'll shoot!" they yell.

The First Mate, towering over us, yells back. "Shoot! Doors steel! Ricochet yourself five times if you want to!"

I help Sara to her feet.

"How did you know?" she says.

I point out the captain's hat.

"What if that's his old one and he left it there years ago?"

"Then we're dead."

I get a look from her I haven't seen before but wouldn't mind seeing all the time.

"You said you weren't a warrior."

"I said we weren't in a war."

One time—once!—in my life, I manage a good comeback at the right time and it almost gets drowned out by the pounding and yelling from behind the watertight hatch.

"What's going on?"

The First Mate smiles apologetically. "We leave a bucket over the door. Slam door close, it falls. Ammonia and bleach. Good for clean floor."

"In a well-ventilated area," Sara says as we hear gasping and feet pounding at the door, more and more weakly—and then silence.

SPIN

-And that's your story? You did it all
to win back the girl?

No, I thought of her in the middle. I did it all for
Prince Rahim.

-Oh please!

Well, he's the one who'll gain from it, one way or the
other. Harry always says, "Take credit." Somebody made it
happen, it might as well be me.

We wait long enough to make sure the soldiers are
good and knocked-out; then the sailors cover their noses and
mouths with handkerchiefs, open the hatches and quickly
remove the guns and ammo. They carry the slowly-reviving
bodies to the brig, where the other twenty or so soldiers are

arrayed on the floor like so many vomiting, moaning bags of laundry.

By the time we meet up with the Captain and climb the main staircase, we're a formidably-armed group. Some sailors stick to one gun while others have confiscated as many as they can carry. I find myself toting up what these guns would be worth if I sold guns—I just can't leave business at the office.

We reach the main deck and peek out into early morning light, the remaining fog burning off quickly. The captain sends scouts, expecting a battle with Dieter and Bossman and the remaining soldiers on the bridge.

Six sailors climb the superstructure around the bridge, prepared to swarm that outpost from all sides. But it isn't necessary.

They immediately wave us up the ladder. We arrive in time for a truly memorable knock-down, drag-out fistfight careening all across the bridge. Dieter curses much more colorfully than Bossman, but Bossman's got a good left. None of his crewmen leave their stations to help him—but they aren't paying much attention to their instruments, either.

Which pretty much explains the ship running aground, a deep shudder followed by a ripping noise way below deck as the *Mercury Venture* slams into the beach. Just in front of the six or seven thousand early birds at the Sunrise Festival.

-You're saying this was just a coincidence.

Not at all. This was Diamante's plan. Pokemon Go.

-Please don't tell me that.

Download a spoofer program yourself and see. While we were all arguing on the bridge and the crew was eliminating soldiers below deck, Diamante plugged his phone in to charge and laid it on top of the GPS unit in the communications rack. His spoofer jams the satellite GPS signal and replaces it with data of its own—just like it does when he's hunting Pokemon. The trick, though, is to make the deception subtle enough that the crew doesn't detect it. In this case, the spoofer just said the ship was off-course by four degrees, which nobody considered a big deal.

-The spoofer made the ship drift to port?

No, it told the instruments that the ship was drifting to port when it *wasn't*. The navigator corrected for it and turned the ship four degrees to *starboard*. Driving it right into the beach at Qumrahdi.

-You're saying he planned all of that?

I told you he was a smart guy. Look, from the moment we reached the ship, this whole thing was improv—I had my plan, he had his. Mine was maybe more haphazard than his.

-It worked out very conveniently for you, though.

I'll admit the location was ideal, coming ashore just as Prince Rahim was on the spot, greeting the eclipse lovers.

-Such convenience suggests design.

Don't look at me like that. I didn't have a phone, I told you. Diamante's was busy spoofing the GPS. And Yusuf was still locked up.

-Your Sara had a phone. As did Princess Amina.

That's true, I suppose. If you want to base your prosecution on women gossiping on their cellphones, be my guest.

As far as I'm concerned, it's a happy coincidence that Rahim happens to be in the right place with your security team, who rush aboard the ship and find the crew holding twenty-some prisoners, a group of American defense contractors and a bigger group in the uniform of the Iranian Revolutionary Guard. You of course secure the bridge, as any effective security force would, arresting Dieter and Bossman and his crew.

-**And you.**

I don't remember anyone ever telling us we were under arrest. You escorted us back here to this compound, after I took Prince Rahim on a tour of the cargo bay.

-**[clears throat] Excuse me?**

Well, you were busy moving the soldiers off the boat and Rahim was absolutely fascinated by the Syrian archaeological treasures and the sixty-five-megaton nuclear device. That one really threw him for a loop.

-**So you're telling me that he received no warning?**

I'm *not* telling you that. I have no idea what happened after we left them all behind. But seriously—if Yusuf warned you that Harry Sandler was threatening your country with a homemade nuclear weapon, would you take that seriously?

In the end, it doesn't matter what he knew then. What matters is what he knows *now*. What also matters is that your security guys took the contractors and the Iranians off the ship in front of cellphone cameras.

-No cameras. We cleared the beach first.

You didn't clear the hotel, did you? Sixty stories of big windows overlooking the site.

-We stripped the soldiers to t-shirts. No one knows who they were.

Right—just a bunch of really buff guys, some in Revolutionary Guard black Kevlar pants and some in American camouflage Kevlar pants, being led away at gunpoint—and a crew in Hazmat suits coming on board. I'll guarantee you fifty good conspiracy theories on YouTube by lunch tomorrow.

-I must say, I don't see that this is good for any of us, you included.

Excuse me. My job is to know the angles. Like I said, if not for this craziness, we'd already be in jail. Instead, we're here, being interrogated by you. Why? Because this is a very big mess in a very public place. Rahim has to give a press conference soon and his answers better be satisfying.

-Which puts you, as they say, on the hot seat.

Au contraire. It puts *you* there.

-I am a servant of my country. To me, this is not a game.

I was a servant of my country until they nailed me to a wall in front of Congress for doing exactly what they told me to do. Of *course*, it's a game! Anything with winners and losers is a game.

-Everything has winners and losers.

Incorrect. Games have winners and losers. Games can be rigged. Games have loopholes, they have favored customers. Real Life is chaos—no rules, no limits—but no loopholes either. *Everybody* pays. Everybody. We all die, don't we? And at that point, all the games are just stupid.

So now, since yes, we're playing a game—let's play smart! Rahim's known me for years—why aren't the two of us having a simple conversation? He wants to be protected from this whole thing—so he's put *you* in the middle.

-I don't—

Don't be stupid. This is an opportunity for you. You've just got to take care of him.

-(pause) I don't need your—

Here's how I see it—you tell me where I'm wrong. Rahim needs a story he can use and your job is to get it for him. Considering the players, your only choice is between Dieter's story and ours.

I'm assuming Dieter's story is that he—an American contractor working in the region—somehow stumbled onto a plot by Harry, Sara, Diamante and me to smuggle a nuclear device and archaeological contraband out of the Gulf and he managed to foil it all by himself. Is that pretty close?

-I said before, you answer questions, not—

I mean, it's the only story he can tell, given what's known. My guess is, he barely spoke to you at all—he just assumed you would cover for him.

-Uh, what makes you think that?

Only everything I know about the guy. And I'm sure you've heard from Parker Meridien already, demanding the fix in Dieter's favor. Because he's one of their protected and I already have a history as a fall guy for Langley. Is that also close?

-(shifting in his seat) Possibly.

Of course it is—that's their whole gig, shoving their cock-and-bull story down your throat because they're the Masters of the Universe.

Except, I think you're going to shove their story back down their throats, because it isn't the story that suits *you* best. Or Rahim.

    `-(pause) Go on.`

The first problem with Dieter's story is that Harry and Sara and I are already known associates of Prince Rahim. The hotel staff and several wealthy citizens of Qumrahdi saw us arrive in a very noticeable and very expensive vintage racing car, announced as a gift to Prince Rahim. An elite group of international bankers were convinced, reluctantly, to share their party space with us, specifically to accommodate close friends of Prince Yusuf. So Dieter's story leaves a sizeable group of influential mouths you'd have to shut somehow and makes Prince Rahim look compromised by the same people you'd be accusing of multiple crimes. You think he's going to like that conclusion?

    `-(cough) Go on.`

And, if you check with your media, I'll bet you some reporter has already found out we arrived yesterday on an American military transport, with no flight plan and no paperwork.

    `-How would someone find that out?`

Maybe women gossiping on their cellphones—who knows?

The point is, if *that* gets to the media, the whole question of undocumented flights blows wide open. Remember the firestorm over the rendition planes? The questions wouldn't only be about Wadiirah—the media would blow it up, like they always do, into a worldwide issue. So Parker Meridien might want to protect Dieter, but I suspect your ally, the US government, wants nothing to do with those types of consequences. You see my point?

-(choking noises) Go on, please.

Okay, the way I see it, we're in the same business— collecting the facts and then telling stories that cover those facts in a useful, though not necessarily truthful, way.

I'm sure Prince Rahim—and therefore, you—will like *our* story much better: Poor unfortunate known associates of the Prince, falsely accused of smuggling a bomb into Paris, discover a forged shipping certificate—I'll forward you a copy as soon as you let us out of here—and trace it to the Gulf. We arrive here and expose a smuggling ring involving a rogue American security contractor, acting entirely on his own, for reasons of personal profit, with a team masquerading as Iranian Revolutionary Guard soldiers. You can say the Hazmat guys were called to the ship because of a faulty air conditioning unit.

    -That's a bit flimsy, don't you think?

How about this, then? I give you access to several bank accounts in Dieter's name and the address of a Russian in Cyprus whose money is in those accounts, on account of, he was supposed to take delivery of the Syrian relics— copies of his shipping certificates are in the ship's manifest. You shake him hard enough, I'll guarantee he'll sell out Dieter in a heartbeat. Once the Americans see him and Dieter in bed together, they'll cut Dieter loose without a breath. But you'll have to deal with the fallout.

    -I don't like that.

You won't. Look, I'm trying to make this easy for you. Go with my story, it's the one Rahim already prefers. And you organizing everything so it all lines up, makes you a very valuable asset for him.

    -How do you know he prefers this story?

Because I ran it by him in the hold of the ship. I told you—you're just a buffer in case something goes wrong. Except nothing's going to go wrong.

-(long pause) You're certain the ship's
captain will back your story?

As certain as I am that the suitcase carrying our
$750,000 is missing.

-Someone could still write about the
transport. And the race car—you bought that
with Dieter's money!

I explained to you how all that happened.

-And if the reporters track down Mr.
Woczynski?

I'll guarantee you, word is already getting around that
Mr. Woczynski used American contractors to loot Syrian
relics; by tomorrow, all the relevant parties will know he
stiffed the Russian mob. In forty-eight hours, *nobody's*
tracking down Mr. Woczynski.

(Silence)

What? That's not enough for you? What's the problem
now?

-There are just a lot of loose ends.

Of course! That's what's real life is—nothing but loose
ends. Thereby providing employment for security chiefs,
spies and public relations executives, in order to provide
something more convenient.

Such as, let the media loose in the hold of that ship. Give them a photo op with Prince Rahim, the heroic ship's crew and you, the head of the valiant security force, posing with the winged bulls and the bust of Alexander. At that point, nobody's going to be worrying the fine print.

THE LAST ACT

And then, within ten minutes, we're gone.

Swept out of the room by a team of muscle boys—close proximity, very clear direction, arms locked below the elbows, which can easily be broken if they're provoked. You move where they move you. You sit the way they tell you to sit. You go to the bathroom and they're knocking on the door every ten seconds, demanding to hear your voice. Where are we going, on an airplane in flight?

This is a *private* jet, ten high-back seats in buttery leather, ours rendered slightly less luxurious by the restraining straps for arms and legs. The crew don't seem to notice—they ask if we want food or drink. Would they feed me if I said 'Yes'? I decide not to find out.

The guards don't talk to you. They pretend they don't speak English. They know it's more intimidating if they say nothing and they're right. They don't read, they watch hunting and fishing shows on the inflight TV and watch the crew with enough distrust that you wonder if assassins aren't seeded just *everywhere* waiting for you. They keep us isolated, different sections of the plane, facing away from one another.

That's when my confidence ebbs away. It was all *braggadocio* anyway but now it just runs out of me like juice from a rotten melon.

I can hear Harry talking at one point—one point that goes on for close to an hour, actually. Pretty interesting too— who knew one geisha caused the Japanese deflation crisis of the 90's? But it's still just talk, without a single reply, so you can't really call it conversation.

As for me, I don't think I've ever spent such a long time without speaking. Just as well—I gave being truthful a shot and it hasn't done a bit of good. Nobody's told us the next step and I'm damned if I'm going to offend anybody before the hearing. Will they give us a hearing? Or was *that* the hearing?

I should be more remorseful. It's not like I did much right, but we came out of it alive, which was the only consistent goal I had. So now I'm exhausted and lost.

Skimming over the checkerboard farmland of Juilly, the last couple of miles before De Gaulle Airport, is one of the saddest moments of my life. I was so looking forward to returning to Paris and now it's surely one of my last moments of freedom.

We pull up to the private airline terminal and the Security boys lead us off the plane, past the gate and out to the airport roadway, where the cabs queue up. We're waiting for a car—but who? The *flics*? *Deuxieme* Bureau? CIA? What are we looking for—a government-issue Escalade? Some generic, invisible-in-traffic Peugeot?

At least they didn't march us off in cuffs—the fact that we're standing here on our own suggests they don't want a fuss, don't want us on the front pages. Does the public know I escaped at all? Did they ever broadcast my face? If they had, they wouldn't leave me on an airport roundabout, would they?

Harry looks surprisingly relaxed. And he should be. I'll plead guilty if they'll leave him alone. I can't imagine him passing the psych test for court anyway.

Sara scans the scene with her reporter's eye and an odd half-smile. I look around and finally notice what's missing. Where have the Security guys gone? The courtyard is full of expensive cars dropping off and picking up customers, people chattering on their way in and out—but nobody with that hollow paranoid eyeflick.

It's a queasy moment, searching for someone you don't want to see, actually getting what you desperately want.

"They've vanished," she says finally. I wouldn't dare.

"What do we do?" I ask.

"Go home," Diamante says.

"They'll say we're attempting to escape."

"If you insist, we can go to a police station and turn ourselves in."

"I'll bet they're not looking for *you*."

"You're so *special*," she snides.

"I'm the man who brought the bomb to Paris."

"I actually *did* try to blow up Saudi Arabia," Harry remarks. "That should count for something."

"If they ask, you don't remember a thing."

"About what? Not a problem. I suggest we eat a fine lunch."

"Harry—"

"What? We're in Paris! We're at large, for the moment, on our own recognizance. Are we *fleeing*, if we tie up for a good bouillabaisse?"

"No."

"Then we might as well go out happy."

We end up at D'Azur, of course, sign for lunch now and pay later, if ever. Harry receives his usual warm welcome and we order every damn thing on the menu.

It's the feast condemned prisoners would eat, let loose in a fine restaurant on an expense account. We're having a lovely time until Millard Hastings hustles in and over to our table.

"Please—don't feel obligated to join us," I say. "Surely there must be some other restaurant willing to charge you full price."

"Ha ha," he says. "You're such a wit." And then he sits down! I know blunt and disagreeable is not my reputation but what does it take to drive him away?

"Honestly—*please* don't join us. Just send the *flics* and I'll hold out my hands for the manacles. But I don't have to eat with you."

He pauses for a moment and takes us in—whatever his secret is, he's actually savoring it, the sadist.

"You don't know, do you?" he smiles, pulling the newspaper from his briefcase and dropping it on the table.

SHOCKWAVES IN WADIIRAH: CROWN PRINCE, 23 OTHERS, PURGED IN 'ANTI-CORRUPTION' MOVE

Qumrahdi, Wadiirah — In a sweeping series of midnight raids, Wadiiran police took 24 leading citizens into custody, including the country's Crown Prince, Ibn bin Salim, its Justice and Defense Ministers, Chief of the National Guard, Chairman of the Royal Broadcast Authority and Haram bin Haram, Wadiirah's best known and most influential financier, owner of Trump Tower Qumrahdi and major investor in Google, Uber and Tinder.

The move was widely seen as a consolidation of power for Prince Rahim

Suleiman Musafa Hattan, nephew of the 86-year-old King Tallah and long-time power behind the throne. Sources close to the Prince, speaking anonymously as they were not cleared to speak to the Press, said the move was focused on "eliminating corruption and a dissident element that has become a cancer at the top level of Wadiirah's elite."

"Irrefutable evidence has emerged," said Colonel Suleiman Qadir, the new Chief of Security, "of a serious plot against the security of the Gulf region, a plot made possible by outsiders seeking influence with sensitive portions of our government. The traitorous element has now been isolated and removed from power."

Rumors spread like wildfire through the capitol this morning, after police retrieved scores of high-ranking officials, conveying them to house arrest in the luxurious Stabler Milton Hotel, of a plot involving rogue security contractors corrupting high-level officials in order to both loot the region of its historic wealth and destabilize Wadiirah, traditionally one of the most secure Gulf states. "I saw the evidence with my own eyes," Prince Yusuf Musaffa Hattan, the new Chairman of the Royal Broadcast Authority and a well-known video blogger in the region, said in a prepared statement.

"I saw the evidence, dog and it was dope!" I say, looking up from the page goggle-eyed. "Wow! Yusuf gets the broadcast authority, Colonel Qadir runs Security and Rahim gets the kingdom."

"He gets the hot seat, more likely," Harry says. "Now he's the boy everyone else is aiming at."

Hastings is smiling. It's just such an unnatural expression, coming from him.

"And what do *you* get out of this, Millard? You seem awfully peppy—I can't imagine Mr. Woczynski is thrilled by all this."

"Ah, there's lots of old junk out there to keep him happy," Hastings dismisses. "In the meantime, we get the contract to investigate the corruption in Wadiirah and rebuild whatever needs rebuilding."

"That sounds wide-ranging," Harry says blithely.

"It sounds lucrative," adds Sara.

"It should be," Hastings says comfortably.

"More to the point, you certainly aren't going to start picking holes in Rahim's story if you're profiting by it."

"That would be ungrateful," Harry says.

"So you've surrendered Dieter to the Gods? The Rogue Security Contractor, I see in the papers?"

"The Rogue Security Contractor is being held incommunicado, I'm told," Hastings says. "Dieter was crucial to capturing him. He is heading our security detail."

"Job security is a wonderful thing."

So far, this is a cynic's wet dream. Nonetheless, this is Hastings—there is surely a twelve-tone chord on the way.

"I just have one little chore left." Here it comes. I notice Harry stirring as well, anticipating the knife.

Hastings turns to Sara. "It's about the wife," he says.

"Am I?" she replies.

"I don't know, are you?" I ask, nervously awaiting her answer.

She stretches in her chair like a cat and throws me a flat-out grin. "We have to make a deal," she says. "I'm just not ready to part with the mattress *and* I still like the apartment, too."

"We can negotiate something," I say.

"Good for you," Hastings says. "My concern is the recent events in Wadiirah. You're not renowned for tact," he tells Sara. This is where we would normally laugh but his tone says 'No'. "You've historically been unable to let sleeping dogs lie, shall we say."

"And you're here to find out if I'll be a good girl."

"You're not known for that either," he smiles, not in a nice way.

"Thank you. What about Harry?"

"He's off his nut, everyone knows that. No one will listen to anything he says."

"Unless I'm calling for the cheque," Harry says. "And Diamante?"

"We assume Diamante will do what you ask."

"I will," Diamante says, fingers moving on phone screen, probably creating a new cybercurrency pegged to the price of bat guano.

"What about me?" I ask.

"Oh, you're the hero," Hastings says, "who tipped everyone off. You discovered the forged shipping certificate. If you hadn't tracked that to the Middle East, we'd never have intercepted the fatal shipment. That's the story—as long as Sara here can be counted on."

Sara takes all this in, nods and raises her hand, taking the oath. "I just want the pony," she says, with as earnest a look as I've ever seen on her face sober.

"No offense, please," Hastings continues, "but how do we know we can believe you?"

"He's speaking in the royal 'we', dear."

"That's because of all those other people behind him," she responds, "waiting for him to get results."

"Pay no attention to the men behind the curtain," Harry mutters.

Sara drapes her arm around Harry's and my shoulders, her two adoring men flanking her. "Harry always gets the last word," she says and puts on her show-announcer voice. "Harry! What's RULE ZERO, the Rule of Rules?"

"RULE ZERO?" I protest. "There's no Rule Zero."

"I didn't have to teach you this one. You knew it already," Harry says, putting down his fork, relishing, as always, the moment and the spotlight and the last word. "It's the old Irish proverb: 'Never let the truth get in the way of a good story.'"

THE END

OTHER BOOKS BY TED KREVER

Mindbenders

Max Renn is a legend of the Soviet mind control program, a genetic experiment, the product of three generations of psychics bred by the state for their power. Before his first mission, the Soviet Union collapses and he disappears.
We meet him twenty years later in the Everglades, keeping as far from people as he can get, until his best friend–his only friend–is murdered and he is forced to assemble a team of people like him to fight the international conspiracy behind the murder.
'...non-stop action...' '...dialog that left me breathless...' '...I couldn't put the book down....finally crawled into bed early hours of the next day...' '...very few books I read that seem as fresh to me as Mindbenders did...' '...an emotional roller-coaster ride...' "Mindbenders...will make you wonder if your mind really does belong to you."

Mindbenders 2: The Fiery Sky

Renn and his Mindbenders team race from a murder-without-clues in Belgium to a floating village in the South China Sea, from an amphitheater in Africa to the Australian Outback, facing a terrifying new opponent who uses Renn's deepest secrets to betray him. Because the most dangerous enemy is the one in your own mind.
'...a more than worthy followup to the first...' '...picks up literally where the first ended...' '...characters are skillfully drawn...' '...intense, memorable scenes...' '...great style and substance...' '...fast paced, well written and exciting!' '...a complete thrill ride...'

GREEN

Paul and Emily have been friends for decades. Emily's beautiful, well-off and has always pursued Paul, in her subtle way. He has never been quite sure why he's not crazy about her. Now, as he hits low ebb, Emily invites him to Ireland, where she trains horses. And Paul wonders, maybe it's time to let her catch me? And then falls for the firebrand Irish barmaid, during international protests against the Iraq War and a chance to turn his whole life around-if he can summon the will to be bold.

'...not your typical romance...' '...a smart, witty and wise look at love later in life ...' '...a unique look into the mindset of men...' '...I found myself laughing aloud more than once, only to shortly thereafter find myself deeply touched.' "The descriptions...of Ireland are alone worth the price of the book..."

A Crafty and Devious God

At the height of the first dotcom boom, when novices were becoming billionaries before lunch and all a girl had to do to be a sensation was take her clothes off now and then, a middle-aged man going through a rancorous divorce gets involved with an Internet exhibitionist. A brilliant and ambitious exhibitionist, determined to gain fame and an IPO -and not above concocting a fictional life story to ensure getting the attention she wants.

"Weirdly excellent" '...an engaging character study...' '...kept reading and reading and reading...' "[The] writing is very natural, loose and easy, yet deep and thoughtful." 'a great read...'

Howling at Wolves

Out of work after 9/11, what would you do? Drive to
Canada to see the girl you were crazy about 25 years earlier-
-but never even kissed--carting along your 77-year-old
former writing professor who can't sit more than two hours
at a clip and swears he's vegan despite the fact that he has a
butcher (with great boobs)? Nearly destroy her business,
bringing Canadian men in touch with their masculinity? End
up in bed with her--and her sister--after being accused of
trying to blow up the Prime Minister with a Super-8
projector? You wouldn't? Well, here's the story of someone
who did.

'This book, simply put...is funny!' "Nothing is sacred..."
'Keep your tissues handy as you won't stop laughing.'
'...like Garp on steroids (or maybe Viagra?)'

After

A collection of short stories written in the post 9/11 era. They
include, among others, a man masquerading in firefighter's
gear in order to get laid, a network news anchor fretting that
his network is the only one not to receive an anthrax threat,
a woman who rented an apartment to one of the 9/11
hijackers and a passenger's widow confronted the next day
by a confused, upset man at her doorstep, covered in chalky
dust and carrying her husband's wallet.

'...a must read...' "...a masterful job of depicting the surreal
dream-like state that trauma survivors inhabit..."
'...intricately woven stories...' a tender tribute to the
survivors of 9/11...'

Author Biography

Ted Krever watched the Beatles on Ed Sullivan, went to Woodstock (the good one), and graduated Sarah Lawrence College with a useless degree in creative writing.

He spent several decades creating programs for ABC News, CBS, CNN, A&E, Court TV, MTV News, Discovery People and CBS/48 Hours, and as VP/Production of a short-lived dotcom.

He has driven a 16-wheeler across the Rockies, shot overnight news in NY City, managed a revival-house movie theater and married twice, in a triumph of optimism.

He was once accused of attempting to blow up Ethel Kennedy with a Super-8 projector.

Read more at www.tedkrever.com